REED CITY

GHOSTI

No generative artificial intelligence (AI) was used in the writing of this work. This story was entirely crafted, with love, by lowly humans.

2026 Ghosti Press

ISBN: 978-1-0674169-0-4

www.iwasghosti.com

1
THE THRILL IS GONE

IT WAS DARK, and Derby O'Malley wasn't sure what he was looking for. Apart from the handlamps he and his associate carried, the only source of light in the massive room was a few thin moonbeams streaming in through a row of small windows, high-up, near the ceiling. The old aircraft hangar had been repurposed as a storage facility. Repurposed and underserved, like most things in The Reeds.

"What do we need?" Derby asked in a hushed voice as they neared the end of a long aisle.

Doc pulled a small note from the pocket of her black hoodie. "Gloves, syringes, and half-inch tubing," she read from the scrap of paper, using the light from her lamp and moving quickly toward the end of the narrow passage. The aisles were very unorganized, sparsely littered with many different types of essential supplies all mixed up on the tall racking. The makeshift facility was being used to store items that were destined for distribution among the various shelters in Reed City; everything from bottled water to nasal spray. Derby stopped, opened his duffel bag, and began sifting through the contents of a nearby shelf, looking for the items that Doc had just listed off.

"No, not from there," Doc said, prompting Derby to give her a puzzled look. She gestured to a large wooden crate that sat near the end of the aisle with the word **AUGUSTA** neatly stenciled in black paint across its side. "From here. This stuff is going to The Uppers." They put down their handlamps and carefully lifted the lid off the crate.

"Won't they notice this stuff is missing?" Derby asked as they began rummaging through the contents of the marked box, pulling out the items they needed and stuffing them into the bags they each carried.

"Nah," Doc shook her head. "They don't need it. I bet they barely open these things," she said, shoving several boxes of disposable nitrile gloves into her open bag. "It's more symbolic than anything. No matter how little we have, they *still* get a chunk. Never forget that, Sticks," she winked, stuffing one last handful of vacuum sealed syringes into the duffel and zipping it up.

'Sticks' was Derby's moniker within the group. Every member of The Bad Moon Crew had one. Doc and her twin brother had given him his, though he wasn't sure why they chose it, and they wouldn't tell him. Like 'Sticks', 'Doc' was also a nickname. Quinn Taylor was the true name of the woman who was now double checking their list against the contents of both open bags to make sure that they had everything. She was shorter than Derby, though he wasn't that tall himself. The small woman's dark hair clawed at the edges of her drawn hood, as though it did not appreciate being trapped and was trying it's very best to break free. On her belt she carried a pair of matching pistols, which you would almost never find her without, and next to one of those was a radio which suddenly flared to life.

BZZT. "How we lookin' in there?"

Doc threw the cross-body strap of the duffel bag over her shoulder and removed the radio from her belt. "Got everything. Still clear outside?"

"Absolutely nothing going on out here, cher." On the other end of the radio, standing watch outside the hangar, was Doc's fraternal twin Marv Taylor; 'The Soulman'.

Doc smirked, "Don't sound so bored. We're coming out." She holstered the radio and with Derby's help, proceeded to carefully replace the lid of the crate.

Derby picked his bag up and followed Doc back down the

aisle. "What do you think the Gamble family needs all these medical supplies for?" he asked, as they made their way in the dark, guided by the soft glow of the handlamps they carried.

"Hell if I know. And I ain't askin. Not our place," Doc said as they made it to the end of the aisle and turned down the walkway, heading past a dozen or so other rows. Each of the aisles was lined with sparsely populated racking, and many were also capped by crates, marked for The Uppers, sitting at their ends.

"C'mon Sticks. You've been with us a few months now, you know how this shit works. The Gambles say jump, we say: How high? How far? And where exactly would you like us to land? And we get it right. And we *definitely* don't ask questions."

The tall, steel doors that separated the storehouse from the world outside loomed ahead of them in the distance. Derby ruffled his closely cut hair, which held a dusty shade of hazel, then drew his hood as if he knew the question he was about to ask was a dangerous one. "I wonder if it has anything to do with Cain Gamble."

"Ha!" Doc turned back, offering him a look that was mostly surprise, tinted by a hint of admiration. "Tell you what, why don't you ask Ruse when we drop this stuff off? I'll make sure to bury whatever pieces of you I can gather." As they were nearing the entrance one of the large doors swung open. Moonlight poured in, illuminating the front area of the hangar, along with it entered a tall man, dressed in a similar black outfit to the other two, though over top of his hoodie, the man wore a long black coat. Just like his twin sister, his dark, wild hair was fighting to escape the confines of his hood.

"Next time, I get the fun job," Marv said, entering the warehouse and leaving the door slightly ajar behind him. "You double check the list?" Marv was the older Taylor twin, by a few minutes, and the circumstances of their youth had caused him to develop a paternal instinct when it came to his sister. Even now that they were grown, that instinct came out from time to time, much to Doc's annoyance.

"Yes, Marv, we got it all," the younger Taylor twin replied exasperatedly, tapping the bag strapped at her side.

Marv put his hands up and his coat opened just enough to reveal the twin pistols that hung in slings at his side. "Alright, just making sure. Remember last time—"

The three members of the Bad Moon Crew stopped abruptly and turned to face the entrance. The sound of a vehicle rolling up on the gravel road outside the warehouse slipped through the slightly open doors, accompanied by a flood of flashing yellow light.

They looked at each other wide-eyed. "Shit. The A's," Doc hissed. The group began to retreat into the facility, turning off their handlamps as they went. The sound of heavy vehicle doors shutting came from outside and muffled voices began to trickle into the warehouse. Derby followed Doc to the left while Marv peeled off to the right as they all scrambled into the depths of the hangar to hide.

"Dammit. Another break-in." A deep voice carried from just outside the entrance.

"We gotta get Ange to double up these locks or something," a softer, higher voice replied.

The voices became clear as the A's entered the building. The yellow lights that still breached the front doors were characteristic of the trucks driven by representatives from The Uppers. They were officially titled Coordinators but 'A's' was the local term of affection, a name which stemmed from the distinctive 'A' patches that were sewn into the sleeves of their uniforms.

Derby followed Doc quietly down a long aisle, carefully navigating the darkness. As they approached the outer wall of the building, he was barely able to make out a small nook in the corner of the building surrounded by a few stacks of what looked like more crates, similar to the one they had been rummaging through a few minutes ago. He tapped Doc on the shoulder, gesturing to the prospective hiding space. The two of them snuck quietly along the wall of the facility and nestled themselves behind the wooden boxes.

"You see they're buildin' a stage in the Drum?" the deeper voice asked. "For Tithe next week."

"I saw." The higher voice sounded annoyed. "A bit performative. Maybe The Fifth should fix some of the problems we have up top before they start building stages. . ."

Derby watched the lights from the lamps that the A's were carrying as they moved further into the depths of the warehouse. Sweat began to bead on Derby's forehead, and his chest rose quick and shallow. He could just barely make out the shape of Doc next to him in the dark, but he could hear the woman calmly breathing through her nose. The Taylor twins, and all the members of the Bad Moon Crew were far more well-adjusted to this type of activity than he was.

The whine of a power tool echoed through the massive room, causing Derby to jump and nervously peek out from their hiding spot. Far in the distance, in the same aisle where the Bad Moons had procured their supplies, he could see the outlines of the two officers. They appeared to be drilling the lid onto the wooden crate that was marked for The Uppers, seemingly unaware that the box was now a fair bit lighter than it had been. After a few minutes they picked up the crate and began walking it out of the aisle.

Derby was pulled, suddenly, back into the nook. Doc's hand was on his shoulder and though the darkness of the hangar obscured her face, he could feel the sternness of her gaze emanating out at him from the shadows. He closed his eyes and worked on controlling his breathing while they sat there in the dark. He wasn't sure how long they hid while the A's secured the crates, carried them out of the storehouse, and placed them into their vehicle. Maybe ten minutes. Maybe twenty. Eventually, they could hear what sounded like the tailgate of a truck slamming shut. The officers, presumably having got what they came for, were preparing to leave.

After a few moments sitting in the relative quiet, Derby got restless. He knew the A's were still nearby, but discomfort in the uncertainty of their whereabouts overwhelmed him. He moved, once again, peeking around the boxes to see if the hangar was clear, and in the dark, he misjudged how close he was to the stack of crates, bumping it just hard enough to knock the lid at the very top loose. It crashed to the ground loudly, echoing throughout the vast warehouse. Derby froze. There was a scramble outside the entrance, and he could see lamplight re-entering the building. He snapped back into the hiding place, breathing heavily once again, his heart thumping in his throat. Doc calmly placed her hand over his mouth, encouraging him to keep quiet.

"Definitely heard something." The deep voice rang clear again through the room and they could hear footsteps, which began moving toward their nook of safety.

"Could be an animal or somethin' got in," the softer voice suggested. The light from the A's lamps was beginning to creep around the wall of boxes at the Bad Moons' backs.

"Or maybe whoever busted the lock off the door is still

here." The deep voice placed the officers right on the other side of the crates now, Derby felt Doc's hand slide off his mouth and down to her hip, preparing for the worst.

"*THE THRILL IS GOOONE AWAY—*"

Music was suddenly blaring from outside the warehouse. It took all of Derby's willpower not to jump and take down the wall that was shielding them. It sounded like it was coming from the radio in the officers' vehicle.

"What in the hell?!" The A's sounded startled as well. The tinny speakers of the vehicle and thin reverberations from the sheeted steel walls of the repurposed hangar did their best to dampen the melody of the song ringing out through the night, but they didn't succeed. The mopey blues pushed through all that adversity and filled the room up anyway. Derby could hear the officers' brisk footsteps pattering away from the nest of crates and back toward the entrance, abandoning their search in light of this new disturbance, arguing as they went.

"Did you leave the keys in there?"

Derby heard a jingle in the distance. "Been on me the whole time. I ain't a moron."

As the A's moved outside their voices became muffled. The doors of the vehicle opened and closed, and the music finally dampened a little. After a few more tense moments in the dark with the remnants of the song floating in the air, they finally heard the vehicle drive off down the gravel road.

"Jesus, Sticks!" Doc smacked Derby hard in the arm and turned her handlamp back on. "You just *can't* sit still, can you?"

Derby turned his lamp on as well. Doc didn't look genuinely mad; she mostly looked relieved. "Just trying to keep you on your toes," he replied, trying to sound brave while his heart still pounded in his chest.

Doc chuckled. "Ah, well. Everyone's alive, that's what matters." She stood, leading them out from their hiding spot. "At least I *hope* we're all good. Marv!" Derby calmed down as they made their way back to the entrance where The Soulman was waiting, leaning against the open hangar door, twirling a small multi-tool around in his hand.

"The Thrill is Gone, BB King, 1969," he said as he pocketed the tool.

"You saved our asses, so I'll forgive the song choice," Doc said as she took the duffel bag off her shoulder and shoved it into Marv's hands, walking past him and out of the building.

Marv smiled. "She hates the blues," he said to Derby as the two of them exited behind Doc out into the cold, clear night.

REED CITY

Part One

The Bad Moon Crew

2
THROUGH DIRT AND BONE

"LISTEN."

The sound of shovels moving soft dirt filled the air in this corner of the sprawling graveyard. "That's the sound of discontentment." Ruse Gamble stood at the edge of the cemetery looking out over Reed City.

The burial grounds were nestled in the hills that bordered the north side of the city. Looking south from here offered an unobstructed view of The Reeds and from this vantage the city looked like a hurricane. The large central market, known as 'The Drum', was the eye, surrounded by a turbulent sea of buildings that was densest near the center but thinned as you approached the edges. If you followed the winding road that blew out north from the storm, into the hills and past the cemetery, you'd find Gamble House. A vast, long-abandoned hospital once funded by the Gamble family. Even further up, at the top of the long slope, the road came to its abrupt end at the doors of a very large elevator, made of tall glass walls. This lift traversed the steep cliff-face between the outskirts of The Reeds, and the city of Augusta, known as 'The Uppers', that sat far above. A trip that no resident of Reed City could take except under very extenuating circumstances.

Ruse turned to the man beside him, cutting the end of a thick cigar with a beautifully engraved silver cigar cutter. "It's pure disdain that drives them, Arthur. Even with a name like mine, getting a man to shovel up a corpse?" He looked down the slope at his crew diligently digging and struck a match to light his cigar. "That's no easy task."

The man standing with Ruse was Arthur Rook. While Ruse was well-dressed, middle-aged and largely unassuming in appearance, Arthur looked like a person you did not want to get on the wrong side of. The man wore all dark and smoke-colored clothing, his hard face made more intimidating by a menacing scar across his left eye. "Sir, I—"

"I know Arthur, *you* would be elbows deep if I asked you. But there's history there, and you're different. These men here tonight? They wouldn't just commit an act like this. No matter who was ordering it." Ruse began to lead the way down the hill toward the dig site, puffing on his cigar. Arthur followed, flipping a short, serrated blade between his fingers as they descended. "They need a reason, something beyond fear or intimidation. Something they resent more than the act that needs committing, and that they can't run from." As Ruse approached the site, the crew stopped digging and stepped back, letting him through to the open grave. "Under those conditions, only one path remains. . .through dirt and bone." He reached into the grave and swept away the loose ground that was still scattered over the dead man's face.

"Take Danny here. He tried to run away from his shitstorm of a life. Tried to escape into oblivion." Ruse now spoke directly to the dead man, as though Danny's corpse could hear him. "Thought you'd find peace in the grave, did ya?" He reached down and pried the man's right arm up through the dirt. "Well, you shoulda known Danny boy," he whispered and, placing Danny's bloodless thumb into the end of his cigar cutter, he leaned in, closer to the corpse than most would hazard, speaking softly. "I always get my pound of flesh."

SNIP. The finger came free with no resistance, and no mess.

"Ruse." A slender, stern-looking woman approached the crowd gathered around the grave. "The Bad Moon Crew is here."

Ruse placed Danny's severed thumb into a small silver box and stepped out of the hole, motioning to the crew who renewed the drone of shovels as they began to refill the man's disturbed resting place. "Good. Bring them up."

They stood at the black iron gates of the cemetery watching the well-dressed woman trudge away between the headstones up the soft slope to where the rest of the Gamble crew was gathered. “We should ask King if we can get a truck or somethin’ in the next couple months. Whatever Buck has at the yard that’s decent.” Doc lit a cigarette and took a drag, the end of the smoke burning brightly in the night.

“We’ve been walkin’ our whole lives Doc, what do we need wheels for now?” The Soulman was doing a final tally of the items in the duffel bags.

Doc shrugged. “Respect? All the respectable groups have vehicles, right?” she replied, taking another drag of her cigarette.

“Do we want respect for a ride, or do we let em keep that?” he said, finishing his count and zipping the bags back up.

“I’m just saying it would be—”

Doc noticed Derby, dazed and staring off into the lower, eastern side of the graveyard. She snapped her fingers. “Sticks, you alright?”

Derby was yanked back into the moment. “Huh? Yeah, sorry. Yeah. I’m good.”

"You were in another dimension there, dude," she said. "You sure you're gonna be okay in here?"

Derby pawed at his neck nervously. "I'll be fine." He checked the watch on his wrist, a classic black and silver timepiece with thin hands and notches for the numbers that organized in such a way to let him know it was just past eight o'clock in the evening. "Why are we dropping off in the cemetery anyway?"

Marv handed one of the bags to Derby. "Because the man said to be here. So, this is where we are."

Derby slung the strap over his shoulder. "Right. No questions."

"Damn straight." The woman had returned. "Let's go, he's ready." She turned back up the slope and the three Bad Moons followed.

Marv walked ahead, falling into stride next to their escort. "Comment va ton frere ce soir?"

The woman's stern exterior cracked just slightly. "Toujours un connard, mais ca devrait aller. . ." They continued to talk as the group headed further up the hill.

Doc leaned toward Derby as they lagged slightly behind the other two. "Marv used to speak French with our parents. Since then, he's only spoken it with Natalia." She nodded toward the pair that walked in front of them. "They were a thing for a while. Fizzled out a year or so back. Probably best, dating a Gamble is dangerous business. They're still friendly though. Marv is just about the only person she seems to tolerate. Aside from Simmons." Just ahead of them, The Soulman made a joke, managing to pry the faintest smile onto Natalia's face. "It's a special thing if you can find it. Someone who can crack your mask like that." Doc turned toward Derby, suddenly wearing a look of regret. "Ah, shit. Sticks, I'm sorry."

Derby smiled. "It's okay."

"Nah, that was insensitive—"

"Really, Doc. It's all good."

"Ah! The Taylor Twins. My favorite Bad Moons." They had reached the lot where the Gamble crew was working and Ruse was there waiting, his arms spread wide in a welcoming gesture and a showy grin on his face. Arthur Rook stood dutifully by his side, as usual. Natalia Gamble left Marv's side and stood between Arthur and a much larger man who had an air of dignity about him. Simmons was the Gamble family attendant. He stood, stoic, in his three-piece suit and removed the pair of round glasses that he wore, wiping them clean with a silk handkerchief he had pulled from his breast pocket before returning them to their perch on the bridge of his nose. Simmons served all the Gambles by title, but in practice the man was Natalia's bodyguard.

"And Mr. O'Malley as well," Ruse said, looking at

Derby. "You've got some work to do to live up to the twins here." He winked.

Derby smiled politely. Marv handed the duffel bag he was carrying to Arthur Rook, and Derby followed his lead. The scarred man opened one of the bags up and tossed the other to Simmons who joined him in taking inventory of the contents.

"Any trouble?" Ruse asked, puffing on his cigar.

"A little hiccup with the A's but we got in and out. No one saw us," Doc replied

Marv smirked. "Besides, wouldn't have been any fun if there wasn't a bit of trouble," he said. Ruse laughed, billowing clouds of grey all around them.

Derby had heard the shovels on their way up the slope which should've clued him in, but being so distracted, it didn't fully hit him until he saw the scene over Ruse's shoulder. One that he couldn't help but stare at: A crew of Gambles plodded away, re-packing recently disturbed soil into a grave.

"Just paying respects." Derby's attention snapped back to Ruse's voice, and he noticed the man, along with the Taylor twins, looking at him. "Paying our respects to a dearly departed friend," Ruse said, staring intently at Derby who nodded nervously in response.

The group continued their conversation, but Derby could only pay half attention. The implication of the activities taking place in the background overwhelmed his mind, and as hard as he tried, he couldn't stop his eyes from drifting back to the scene unfolding behind the group.

Derby grunted as Doc nudged him hard in the ribs and he realized that Ruse was once again looking at him, now with dark amusement.

"It's all here." Arthur and Simmons had finished counting the items.

"Good," Ruse said, not taking his eyes off Derby. "Why don't you two help Arthur load up the van." He gestured to the Taylor twins. "I'd like to have a chat with Mr. O'Malley here."

"Sure thing." Doc shot a look of concern back at Derby as her and Marv picked up the duffel bags and followed Arthur to the van. Ruse turned, heading silently up the hill to the overlook at the edge of the cemetery. Derby followed, his face hot with anxiety as he moved through the trail of smoke that traced the Gamble leader's path. When they reached the top, Ruse leaned on the low fence and took a deep drag of his cigar.

"Derby O'Malley. King's newest Bad Moon." He was looking Derby straight in the eyes, tendrils of thick grey running out of his nose. "Tell me about yourself."

"Me? I uh—" Derby stammered; his nerves clear in his voice.

"It's okay kid, you can relax. You're not in danger."

Derby took a deep breath in through his nose and composed himself. “Temporary Bad Moon.”

Ruse’s eyebrows rose slightly. “Temporary?”

Derby nodded. “The crew is giving me a place while I. . .figure things out.”

“Ah.” Ruse took another long drag of his cigar. “I heard about your loss. Girlfriend, was it?”

Derby lowered his gaze.

“Rough, that.”

It sounded sincere which made Derby feel a little more comfortable. He brought his eyes back up and looked out at the city that sprawled below them. “This place feels haunted for me now, I guess. Or maybe *by* me, I—” He shook his head, remembering where he was, and cleared his throat. “Anyway, it’s a nice thing King’s doing, putting me up, but he knows I’m getting out of here as soon as I can, so I’m just trying to be helpful in the meantime.”

Ruse looked intrigued. “Leaving The Reeds? Not many options there. Where to?”

Derby shrugged. “The Uppers.”

Ruse let out an emphatic chuckle. “Derby O’Malley! You ambitious little tragedy.” He looked the young man up and down. “I respect that.” Ruse turned, leaning with his back to the fence now and looked away from the city, up the hills to the north, puffing on his cigar. He pointed to the top of the northern cliff, where the back side of a big industrial facility could be seen cresting over the edge. "Do you know what that building is?"

The facility was just a short distance away from where the tall glass elevator surfaced into The Uppers. Derby knew what it was. "The Hydro?"

Ruse nodded slowly. "You know how it works?" he asked.

Derby shook his head.

"All the runoff from The Uppers funnels into that building. Their used water gets treated and sterilized in there and then gets piped down here for redistribution." He paused. "We're drinking their *shit*, son." There was a hint of true disdain in Ruse's voice. Derby wasn't sure what to say. Ruse cracked a smile. "I guess I can't blame you for wanting to be on the other side of that transaction."

"I—" As Derby began to speak, Ruse put his hand calmly but heavily on the young man's shoulder, and he knew not to continue.

"I'm rootin' for ya, kid. I like the gusto." His hand gripped Derby's shoulder a bit tighter, and he looked him straight in the eyes, demanding his gaze, almost daring him to look anywhere else. "But for the time being, while you're still rollin' around in the muck with us dogs, make sure you learn your leash."

Ruse released his grip, patted Derby's arm and gave him a nod that clearly signaled: 'Leave'. Derby made his way down to the Taylor twins, legs feeling hollow and Ruse's message clear in his mind.

Reed City was a low place. Low in most every measurable sense. It was low in status, in altitude, even the infrastructure never got too ambitious, with no building standing higher than three stories. The place had humility built into its very foundation. The one area where The Reeds dared to reach was in spirit. It was a loud place. Loud in all ways. Amidst the neon and the noise and the many rows of buildings that made up the center of the city, nestled in the top corner of an apartment, was the home of The Bad Moon Crew.

DING. The twins and Derby exited the elevator into the third-floor hallway. As they approached the door to unit 315, a welcoming cacophony of music and voices was seeping through the frame. Doc scanned her fingerprint on the panel next to the door, and the lock clicked open.

As they entered the apartment, they were greeted by the wash of music playing, and a scene in the kitchen. "No! You're drowning it!" A young girl was perched on the countertop next to the stove where there stood a very large man throwing various ingredients into a cavernous pot. A woman sat at the small dining table behind them watching the scene with a smile.

"Chill, little one. I've done this before," the man said.

"Ya, and it's always too saucy!" the girl shrieked from the counter.

"Ay, they have returned," said the woman at the table as they closed the door behind them. This was the rest of the Bad Moon Crew.

"Welcome back, guys. King's ruining some perfectly good pork." Jen 'JT' Travino was the girl crouched on the counter overseeing the dinner preparations and was the youngest Bad Moon.

"JT, are you questioning the big man's skills?" Marv asked, walking into the kitchen and giving her a one-armed hug.

"To be fair, he did burn the chicken last week," Marisha 'Maman' Igwe chimed in from the table. She was King's longtime partner and second in command.

"Yep, and now he's drowning the pork," JT chirped.

Obo 'King' Kalima, leader of The Bad Moon Crew, laughed a hearty laugh as he stirred the contents of the pot.

"You'll see little one, just trust me," he said, tapping the side of her nose with his thick finger.

Doc and Derby joined Marisha at the table. "JT, off the counter please," the older woman asked kindly. The young girl acted as if she'd heard nothing and continued about her business of interrogating their dinner. Marisha shook her head and turned to the two of them. "How'd it go?"

"Good. Gambles were happy," Doc replied. Marv had begun setting out plates and utensils around the large dining table.

Marisha started, "And you took from the—"

"Yes, Maman. We took from the boxes," Doc finished cheekily, as she got up and began to lay out the food. King loaded up a long plate with a huge pile of delicious looking pork strips. He pointed at the floor and JT jumped down from her perch on the counter, taking a seat at the table. The big man placed the platter of meat in the center of the group, the light catching the dark crest on his hand, just below his knuckles. Each member of the Bad Moon Crew had a tattoo on the back of their right hand, a small, dark illustration. King brandished a simple crown while Marisha wore an ornate sun. A two-tone pill decorated the back of Doc's hand, and Marv's bore the shape of a vinyl record. JT's tattoo was the smallest with her stylized initials sitting in the elbow of the 'L' formed by her thumb and index finger. Derby couldn't imagine burying ink down into his skin, where he couldn't get it out.

"Sticks got a talking to from Ruse," Doc piped up as she took her seat.

"Did he really?" King asked with a grin.

JT looked at Derby. "Oo what was it?" She contorted her face to look stern. 'Remember your place,' she said in her best impression of Ruse Gamble. The group chuckled.

"'Learn your leash,' actually," Derby said seriously.

"Oh, he's getting creative now!" JT said as she took a helping of pork from the serving dish and passed it along.

King patted Derby on the back, handing him a bun from the bowl as he went around the table. "Don't worry too much. Ruse is more bark than bite."

Marisha looked concerned. "I don't know, Obo. The past few months, since Cain has been out of the picture. . .since Ruse took over, he's been different. He feels dangerous."

"Ay, I clocked that too," Marv agreed.

"Bah, the most dangerous thing I can think of right now is how empty my stomach is," King said boisterously as he sat down. He shared a quick look of acknowledgement with Marisha, and they began eating.

"Dammit!" JT slammed the table with her fist as she took her first bite. "This is delicious. You're a genius."

Derby couldn't help but laugh along with the group.

"Oho, look at that! Even in the wake of Ruse Gamble's wrath, he smiles," King said, looking at Derby approvingly. "That's that Bad Moon soul."

Laughter and music carried them through dinner and into the rest of the evening where they blocked out the world in their little corner of The Reeds.

3
FOR A DAY OR A DECADE

IT WAS A PLEASANT DAY on Padre Buck's dusty acreage near the edge of the city's south side. The gruff, elderly man thrust a clipboard into Derby's hands and growled. "I need a signature there, kid."

"Oh, I—Marv?"

"Got it." Marv hopped down from the back of an unmarked box truck. The truck was full up to the door with contents they had just finished transferring from a shipping container that sat open on the rocky lot; one of many that crowded the area. The one they had been emptying was painted black with two crude yellow half-moons sprayed on each long side. Buck looked after the box for the Bad Moons, which they used as a place to store their valuables or items they didn't have space for in the city. He did the same for some of the other groups in The Reeds, as indicated by the various colorful containers strewn across his lot, ownership of each box noted by its unique paintjob. It was impressive that a man of his age was able to keep such good track of what came in and what went out for so many groups. One couldn't be blamed for questioning his capabilities as a caretaker, but King trusted Buck, so he was to be trusted.

"How's business these days Buck?" Marv asked, wiping a fresh layer of sweat from his brow. While The Soulman signed out the items and talked to the old man, Derby drew down the roll-up door on the back of the truck and locked it.

"Storage is always good. Everyone down here, all crammed in, not enough space for everything, I give 'em some." The man paused a moment to spit some thick, brown tobacco residue into an aluminum can he carried. "Autos has been a bit dry late." In addition to managing the many containers sitting out front of the small trailer where he lived, Buck also traded vehicles from the lot at the back of his property. "You ain't the only ones been picking up big last while, this for them Uppers pricks I gather?" the old man asked as he closed and locked up the Bad Moons' black container.

"Ay, it's that time of year again Padre. The Fifth comes down, takes their cut and calls us lucky."

"Bah. Spit in my face and call it rain, may as well." Buck

cackled making another entry into his handheld spittoon. "Anyway, Tav'll drive the stuff wherever you need. Take care."

Marv nodded, handing the pen and clipboard back with his signature on the sheet. "Thanks Buck, we'll catch ya," he called out as the old man retired into his trailer.

Derby walked up to the front of the truck where Tav sat in the driver's seat with the window down. "Where to?" the wiry man asked. The entire cabin next to him was filled with items that they hadn't been able to fit in the back, leaving no room for the Bad Moons to ride along.

"The Drum. We'll meet you down there," Derby said, taking a swig of water from his bottle. The man nodded and drove off. Derby took another short sip and returned the bottle to his backpack. The two Bad Moons started their long walk back into the city, the beating sun of the morning doing a better job of draining Derby's energy as it rose higher in the sky. "You wish we had a truck now?" he asked Marv with a smile.

Marv chuckled. "Naw Sticks, we only get so much light down here. When it decides to shine, I ain't tryin to hide from it."

The streets of The Reeds were lively, only becoming more so as the morning got late and they crossed over the Kin Line, heading north, getting closer to the center of the city. The Kin

Line was an invisible division, existing only in the collective consciousness of the people, that ran across Reed City from east to west, loosely following Kin Street which spanned almost the whole downtown core. The general fortunes of people tended to be higher on the north end of the city and began to plummet as you crossed south of the Kin Line.

"You can do stuff like that ya know," Marv said as they wove their way through a crowd that was gathered out front of a bakery.

"Hm?"

"Back at Buck's. Signing out the pickup. King trusts you, Sticks." They turned the corner leaving the bustling main road for a much quieter street.

"I know, but if I overstep, or do the wrong thing. . .and then I'm just—"

"You're just passing through, ya, but here for a day or a decade you're a Bad Moon. You should own that."

Derby suddenly realized where they were and stopped dead in his tracks. "No." He was distracted and hadn't noticed which route they had been taking into the city.

"Whoa, no need to—"

"No, not that, we can't go this way." Derby stood still, his wide eyes darting around the lane.

Marv looked at him with a unique blend of confusion and concern "What? Paisley Street? But The Drum is just—"

"I know, but *I* can't go this way. We have to go around."

Paisley Street was sleepy and unremarkable, nothing more than a few shopkeepers sweeping their storefronts. Concern flashed across Marv's face. "Sticks, you alright? What's—"

"Marv, just. . .*please*." Derby knew how desperate he looked. He didn't care.

"Okay, okay. We can cut down Fike I guess," The Soulman said, concern still lingering in his eyes.

Relief flooded Derby's body, and he followed the older Taylor twin as they backtracked to the busier street and turned onto it once again, heading toward the alternate route.

Derby felt the tension in his muscles release and his mind begin to calm as they moved farther away from the street that sparked his panic. He broke the silence after a few minutes. "Thanks."

"I got you." Marv looked back at Derby thoughtfully. "If you need anything Sticks, if I can help at all. Or if you just need to talk. . ."

Derby knew the offer was not just a way to ease the awkward tension, it was genuine. He nodded and they continued in silence the rest of the way.

The Drum was a sizable open market swirling at the center of the storm that was The Reeds. A wide-open space flanked at its perimeter by premier shops and specialty kiosks. Three gigantic screens craned over the area like long-necked caretakers, transmitting a cycle of advertisements and a round-the-clock Reed City news broadcast. The market played host to all the city's leading providers of essentials like food, clothing, and other necessities. A furious whirlpool of sights, sounds, and smells; at any given time, The Drum was the most vivid and vibrant part of the city. That was true this week more than any other.

The very center of the market was usually a space left open for patrons to mingle, but today, that space was mostly commandeered by a half-built stage. Once a year, the elected officials from The Uppers, The Fifth Council, would come down to Reed City. They visited under the guise of charity, to show themselves in the community and 'give back' by sharing a few trinkets, but the true purpose of the ordeal was for them to oversee the payment of the annual Tithe. This year, they requested a stage be built for the occasion.

The rest of the Bad Moon Crew were already at The Drum and by the time Derby and Marv arrived, they had finished unloading everything from the truck into the Tithe collection crate that lay heavy beside Aunt Chel's shop at the eastern edge of the market.

"Good to go." Derby patted the side of the box truck to signal to the driver that he could leave. Tav tipped his hat and drove off slowly down the busy street. King and the Bad Moons spent the rest of the morning and the afternoon helping with the stage assembly, an effort that was being led by King's friend Jeph and his crew The Black Ashes, with most other groups chipping in. By the time sunset had cast a warm glow over the market, and they were packing up for the day, the makeshift platform was looking nearly complete.

"Not too bad, ay?" King said, hopping off the stage, joining Marv and Derby and turning to admire the day's work. The fading daylight battled the rising glow of the city behind the big platform. It did look impressive.

"Ay, not bad. Those gits'll feel *real* important up there," Marv smirked.

"We can only hope," Jeph said in his creaky, tattered voice, chuckling as he approached the group. King shook the man's hand firmly and the other two Bad Moons followed suit. "Thank you, for all your help with this," Jeph said, taking a drag from a unique cigarette, one like Derby had never seen before. When the man inhaled, the end burned orange, like any smoke, but the rest of the cigarette was pitch black all the way down, from ash to filter, and the smoke that snaked its way out of his nostrils, was equally dark.

Jeph was dressed in his usual black suit, black tie combination as was customary for members of The Black Ashes. The uniform made the stark pale skin of his face and shaved head stand out even more. The black paint on his fingernails had the same effect on the man's white hands, almost as if his exposed parts were floating, separate from the rest of his body.

King waved his friend off. "Least we could do, Jeph. Besides, everyone's pitchin' in."

"Why do you think that is?" the pale man asked. "They look up to you King, your crew sets an example. I'm grateful for that." Jeph considered the Bad Moon leader for a moment. "You had a chance to talk with Ruse yet?"

King shook his head. "The crew did a drop off for him last night, but we haven't had a chance to sit down."

"Way he tells it, you're a difficult man to schedule," Jeph croaked. King smiled in response. A member of the Ashes called out to Jeph from across The Drum and he began to walk away. "Sit down with him King. Hear him out. Like I said, you're an example." Jeph smiled as he turned and disappeared into the bustle of the crowd.

Derby and Marv decided not to pry and followed King in silence as they all headed over to Aunt Chel's place, joining Marisha and the rest of the group.

Chel was a friendly, doddering woman who ran what was likely the most popular shop in The Reeds. It wasn't that way because she sold anything special, but more that the woman herself was a sort of matriarch for the city. When people needed help, they'd go to Aunt Chel.

"Damn, lots of space left to fill in five days. The Gambles drop off yet?" King asked as they approached the group gathered around the open crate, which was only about two-thirds full.

"Gambles ain't in this year," Aunt Chel replied, sounding despondent. "Ruse sent a note last night. First time I can remember a crew opting out of Tithe, and I been organizing for forty-five years." She shook her head in disappointment. "Especially the damn Gambles."

"Pricks," JT said.

"JT, careful," Marisha warned.

King ran his hands through his hair. "Shit." He took a moment to think. "Alright, we can buck up some more."

"What!" JT squawked. "Fuck that! They're the biggest crew in the city!"

"JT! Lower your voice." Marisha looked around the market cautiously.

"She's right, Maman," Marv said.

"It's bullshit," Doc agreed.

"Listen, I'll meet with Ruse, and we'll sort it with the Gambles later but for now, we figure it out," King said. "I'll talk to Jeph and Eri, I'm sure the Ashes and Leviathan can swing a bit bigger as well. We'll cover it, Chel," he said, placing his hand on the older woman's shoulder and looking at his crew. "We'll be fine."

As much as the Bad Moons wanted to protest, they found themselves comfortably trusting that they would, indeed, be fine. Because King's word was good.

"Thank the Lord for you, Obo Kalima," Aunt Chel said, leaning into him for a brief embrace. As night fully took over, and the city began to glow with the colorful bloom of signs and screens, they helped the woman lock the big crate back up. The crew said their goodbyes and began to leave. "Oh wait, Maman, I'm making a list of volunteers for Feast next month. I need to know which of your crew I can put down," Chel said.

"Just the five of us, Chel. Like usual."

Derby turned around. "You can put me down too." Marisha looked at him surprised. "If you want me there, I mean—"

"Of course, Sticks," Marisha said, maintaining her surprise for another moment and then smiling at him. "Make that six then."

Aunt Chel added Derby's name to her list and The Bad Moon Crew headed home, leaving the emerging nightlife of the Drum behind.

POP. POP. POP.

“Damn, Doc.” A mouthwatering smell filled the air and mingled with the soothing sounds coming from the radio in the home of the Bad Moons as dinner preparations were underway. They didn’t have an abundance of room in the apartment, but they made good use of what they did have. The space that divided the kitchen and the narrow hallway that led to the bedrooms was a large area that served, in essence, as a collection of ways to spend time.

A billiards table with a faded, wine-red felt surface sat in front of a wide and flat television. The TV was showing the same news that was broadcast on the large screens in The Drum; the only channel that anyone had access to in the city. Across the room, directly opposite the television, was the source of the sultry sounds floating through the apartment. A HAM radio rested on top of a tall end table. It was playing music from the 7.15 MHz frequency which projected effortlessly across the room from its place in the corner. The wall next to the radio turned to glass after a short distance; a sliding door that led to a small balcony.

Finally, next to the billiards table, there was a long lane, at the end of which a series of targets were hung. Everyone in the crew had basic firearm skills, it was a necessity of living in The Reeds, but Doc was truly talented.

POP. POP. The rubber bullets snapped out of the dummy pistols and found their mark perfectly. "Remind me to never get on your bad side," Derby said, genuinely impressed.

She smiled at him. "I'd be sharper if I wasn't being lulled to sleep by whatever the *hell* song this is." As if on cue, the calming, slow tune faded out and something new began.

Marv chimed in without looking up from the portable radio he was tinkering with. "Blam!, The Brothers Johnson, 1978."

"Now *this* is more like it." Doc grinned and returned, with renewed energy, to her artful dance. *POP. POP. POP. POP.*

JT was mostly oblivious to all the activity in the house, sitting cross-legged on top of the pool table watching the twenty-four-hour news at point blank range. This is where you'd find the girl most mornings and, on some evenings, like this one.

BZZT. "Bad Moons, this is Natalia Gamble."

The woman's voice sounded out from the HAM radio in the corner, cutting over the music. Marv put down the portable, pocketed his multi-tool, and walked over to the HAM, picking up the handheld transmitter. "Bonjour Nat."

"*. . .Hello Marv. Aunt Chel has your payment for last night. You can pick it up from her when it's convenient for you.*"

"So formal, cher." The Soulman sat down in a nearby chair and threw his legs up on the windowsill, looking out into the night. "Que fais-tu ce beau soir?"

"*Est ce beau? Je ne pouvoir pas dire,*" Nat responded with a begrudging tone. The woman's defense eroded after a minute or two and allowed them to continue amicably back and forth, their conversation backed up by the music that was still playing over the frequency. Derby wasn't sure why things hadn't worked out between them, but it was obvious that something was still there.

"JT!" Marisha called out from the kitchen. The youngest Bad Moon had a pair of headphones plugged into the television and was completely absorbed.

"JT!" Marisha shouted a little louder.

"She's got headphones on," Derby said walking into the kitchen.

"I need her to run to the shop. *Someone* told me we had onions, and we are, in fact, onion-less," she said looking sideways at King who was chopping garlic at the other end of the counter.

"That's just pure slander," King shot back cheekily. "I thought you said *garlic,* of which we have plenty," he said gesturing to the many cloves that littered his cutting board.

Marisha laughed. "Well then, it seems you're growing hard of hearing in your old age." She said the last two words with a playful bite.

King put down his chopping knife and mimed driving an invisible one into his own heart.

"I can go," Derby said.

"Bless, that would be lovely, Sticks." Marisha opened a nearby drawer and brought out a small brown bag from which she extracted a few coins that she handed to him.

"Three onions from the shop down on Ellis would be beautiful."

He opened the apartment door and turned back. "So, three cloves of garlic from the shop on—" King let out a hearty laugh and Marisha shook her head tossing a bit of spinach at him as he left.

The walk down to Ellis Street was not a long one, but those few blocks were enough to make Derby regret not wearing a jacket. It was that time of year where even when the days were warm, the nights were beginning to carry a chill that cut deep. As he approached the dingy little shop on the corner, he noticed a black van parked across the street. It was a Gamble van. Vehicles were not very common in the city, mostly driven by the important groups, so the ones that were around became quite distinct. The Gambles were the only crew he knew of that had black passenger vans like the one parked on the other side of the road.

Derby entered the shop, smiled at the woman behind the counter and headed for the onions at the back. Since the Gambles usually kept to the north side of the city, he found himself wondering what brought them to the center tonight. His step quickened slightly as he made his way up to the counter and paid for his items.

Abandoning the brief, warm reprieve of the little market for the cold pavement of the street, Derby no longer saw the van across the way. Relaxing a little, he turned to walk back toward the apartment and froze. The black vehicle was parked not ten feet in front of him, and he could make out two figures sitting in the front seats. On the sidewalk next to the van, leaning against the stained brick of the adjacent building and dragging on a cigarette, was Arthur Rook. The severe man flanked the mouth of an alley that ran behind the shop.

Arthur nodded at Derby, and he knew. He couldn't just walk past them. He couldn't run. They were there for him. He knew. So, he approached the alley slowly and when he got close, Arthur gestured with his cigarette, imploring him down the dark passage.

Heart firmly in his throat, Derby entered the alley, trying to maintain an air of confidence but gripping his bag of onions tightly. The dimly lit shape of a man stood about halfway down the walk and suddenly, the fiery glow of a cigar lit up, revealing the face of Ruse Gamble.

"Apologies for the theatrics Mr. O'Malley."

"Mr. Gamble." Derby nodded, doing a decent job of feigning confidence.

"I wanted to speak with you in private."

Derby had learned from their last interaction that this was not intended to be a real conversation, so he deferred. "How can I help?"

"Oh, quite the contrary son. You mentioned the other night that you're interested in getting to The Uppers." The tiny fire at the end of Ruse's cigar lit up his face again, momentarily. "I might be able to help with that."

Confusion and interest began to augment the fear Derby felt as he listened.

"I respect ambition, Mr. O'Malley. I owe a lot to it. So, when I find the embers of it in someone like you, I feel a responsibility to stoke them." Derby couldn't help but feel like he was waiting for the other shoe to drop. "Getting out of The Reeds is no easy task. I'd need to pull a lot of strings to make that happen for you. And while I owe a lot to ambition, I can't say the same for charity."

There it was. "You'll help me, if I help you," Derby said.

Another spark of the cigar. "Smart kid. I don't need much. Just a little job. Much like what you did for me the other night. The key to this one is it *has* to stay between us and *only* us."

"What about Ki—"

"No. No Bad Moon involvement. If you talk to *anyone* else about this, the deal's off." The orange glow illuminated Ruse's face once more as he took a deep drag of his cigar; the man's hungry eyes reflecting the light and punctuating his intimidating silhouette. "It's for their own good kid." Ruse's figure, which should have been blurred by the dark of the alley, seemed to be outlined against it instead, by a strange blue hue that bounced softly off the wall behind him. Curiosity implored Derby to scan the area for the source of the cool light, but the man's stare commanded his full attention.

"You see, I'm doing my own dance with ambition here, and it's been *my* experience that the harder you push on the world the harder the world will snap back. The Bad Moon Crew don't want no part of that. Agreed?"

Derby nodded stiffly.

Ruse exhaled a plume of smoke, and the strange glow subsided, his shape blending back into the night. "Good. Besides, it's much easier for me to protect one of you than all of them. You wanna do the impossible kid? Get out of this shithole? Well, you're gonna have to flirt with danger."

Ruse reached into his pocket, pulled something out and placed it into Derby's hand. He could just barely make out what it was in the dim alley. It was a brik. He flipped it open, and the little screen dispersed the dark around it, protesting the stillness of the night. Briks were extremely rare in The Reeds. Derby had seen them but never used one before. Ruse reached over and closed it. "Arthur will reach out to you on that with the details." He walked back toward the mouth of the alley.

Derby followed, his mind a swirl of quarreling thoughts. They reached the light of the street proper, and Arthur opened the sliding side door of the van for Ruse to get in.

"What if I don't?" Derby blurted out; his counterfeit confidence now completely dismantled. "What if I don't...do it?"

Ruse looked at him and shrugged. "It's up to you, son. I ain't gonna kill ya if that's what you're worried about." He got halfway into the van and turned back taking a long inhale of his cigar and looking Derby straight in the eye. "But this fuckin' city might." Arthur followed Ruse into the van, the door snapped shut behind them, and the black vehicle sped off.

The walk back to the apartment was cold and it was slow. Derby felt heavy, weighed down by uncertainty and fear. Weighed down by the brik. An object which felt about as heavy as its namesake in his pocket as he made his way back to the Bad Moons.

4
SOMETHING THAT I CAN'T GIVE AWAY

IT WAS AN UNCOMFORTABLE feeling. Like swimming through the air. A heavy blanket thrown over each of his senses, muting his interaction with the world, as if he was stranded in his shadow. Derby drifted through most of the evening this way, hovering over his own shoulder, preoccupied with thoughts of Ruse Gamble, The Uppers, and the brik in his pocket. Presumably, his body didn't betray him through dinner or the revelry that followed, as none of the Bad Moons seemed to notice that anything was amiss. Or if they did, it raised no alarms. But at some point, later in the night, the anesthetic of shock wore off, and the world was suddenly very loud.

"NO WAY!"

Derby winced.

Marv was currently beating JT in a game of eight ball, much to her very vocal protest. "How are you this good?"

The Soulman lined up his final shot. "*That's* your problem, cher. You're thinking too much about how I'm winning." He struck the cue ball with a gentle precision, and it flew across the table knocking the black ball at a sharp angle straight into the pocket he had pointed to moments earlier. "Instead of focusing on how you're losing." He gave the girl a smug wink, adding insult to injury.

"Oh, blah, blah dude," she said with a giggle as Marv ruffled her hair. "You got next, Sticks?" JT asked, laying her cue down on the red felt.

"Hm? Oh, no thanks." Derby was starting to wear the stress on his face. "I think I might turn in actually. Feeling kinda rough."

"That sucks, dude. Feel better then," Doc said, smiling at him as she picked up the cue and re-racked the table.

Derby stood, hoping some sleep would clear things up. On his way to the narrow hall that led to the bedrooms, he noticed King sitting out on the balcony by himself, exhaling a dense, grey cloud into the air. He turned from the hallway and walked to the balcony door, not a hundred percent sure why or what he was going to say, but his legs carried him there regardless.

"Sticks!" King looked up with surprise as Derby slid the glass door open and closed it shut behind him, stepping out into the brisk air. "Have a seat." The big man gestured to the empty chair beside him and Derby sat down, taking in the view for a moment, letting his nerves calm.

The apartment balcony provided a well-framed scene of the north side of the city. The luminous color of The Drum glowed brightly to the northwest, beyond which the city spread out and dimmed as it approached the hills in the north. The towering structure that ferried the broad glass elevator through the sharp cliffs between The Uppers and The Reeds loomed behind the city, an admonishing backdrop, and just below it the gothic shaped buildings that comprised Gamble House stood silhouetted, their windows lit up like tiny fires in the night.

Derby spoke into the silence. "Been a few months since that place lit back up. Before that, I only ever remember it being dark." He paused, breathing in the cold night. "My whole life I saw Gamble House hanging over the city, abandoned, like a. . .like a reminder." He shifted in his seat. "Then Cain Gamble goes missing and all of a sudden, there's life there." A few moments passed and silence threatened to encroach on them again, King billowed more grey clouds into the air. "It has to be related, right?" Derby asked.

King nodded slowly. “Could be, Sticks.”

“Maybe he got sick or something and they’re treating him there?”

King smirked.

Derby sat back in his chair. “Seemed like you two were close.”

The smirk faded. “Ay, we ran deep. Long as I can remember.”

“Are you worried about him?”

“Course I am.” King paused, staring thoughtfully out into the hills, then, turned to Derby with a smile. “No use worrying tonight though. I hear you asked Maman to put your name down for Feast with us next month.”

Derby nodded. “I did.”

“That mean you’re gonna be sticking around a while?”

“I think so.” He felt the brik, heavy in his pocket. “I don’t know. Listen, King, I’m sorry.”

“What for?”

“I. . .” Derby wasn’t sure what he was going to say next. “When I went out tonight, to the shop, I. . .I was thinking about everything you and the crew have done for me the past few months and I’m really grateful.” He leaned forward in his chair. “But this place, man.” He stared out at the sprawling city.

"Every day I'm just wading through painful memories and the longer I'm trudging through it the slower I move, the deeper it all soaks into me." He paused, looking distant. "And I can't wash it off. I've tried, but it just. . .it's too deep. I don't know where to go from here except away. Far as I can." He took a breath. "If I get an opportunity for that, for a fresh start, I *have* to take it." He looked at King apologetically. "I guess that's what I'm sorry for."

King shook his head. "No need to apologize for that. Sounds like a nightmare, true and through." He extinguished his smoke in a little ceramic tray on the table between them. "'Sides, you were honest about that up front. Wherever you end up, Sticks, I hope you find your peace. And you know you *always* have a place here. That's what this crew is, brother. A place. For people who lost theirs. And once you're in, you're in."

"For a day or a decade," Derby said slowly.

King smiled. "That's right. Marv left for a while, you know. Found his way back."

"Really?"

King nodded. "Couple years ago. Him and Nat Gamble decided they wanted to try and make it work on their own. Big respect to them. A story that ain't mine to tell but in the end, they went their separate ways, and Marv was left owing the Gambles a few hundred coin." He chuckled.

Derby sighed. "You really can't catch any type of luck in this place, other than the shit kind."

King shook his head. "Nah, luck is small Sticks. It's consequence. Somebody's anyway, that's what most of it is. And us Bad Moons, we share each other's consequence, the good and the bad. Besides, Cain cut that debt down to something manageable for us. No sweat. And we were glad to have The Soulman back."

"I'm sure he was glad too. You're good people." Derby stood up from his chair and walked back to the sliding door leading into the warm apartment.

"I hope you find what you're lookin' for, Sticks," King said. "And if you can't find a way to wash that pain off, maybe you can let it sink in, wear it, like ink." The big man smiled, and Derby could see why King was so trusted, why people looked to him as an example. There was something genuine behind his eyes, something that you couldn't fake. Whatever the man was saying, whatever advice he was giving, he truly believed it was the right thing.

Derby nodded. "Goodnight, King." He closed the door behind him, leaving the Bad Moon leader on the balcony, and retreated, past the lively billiards game still playing out in the rec area, down the narrow hallway to his bed, where he tried to fall asleep with a typhoon in his mind.

CREAK. The heavy steel door opened slowly, taking their combined effort to move. The drafty inside of the building was covered with dirt that had blown in between the boards nailed across the windows over the many years it had been left deserted.

"Place hasn't changed a bit," Doc said, looking around the empty room before turning back and helping Derby close the solid door behind them. *CLANG.* The dilapidated building they were in was deep in the southern extremities of the city. No one living in the Reeds had it easy, but the going got markedly tougher the further south you ventured. They had moved carefully on their way down here, especially once they got below the Kin Line. Desperation had a chokehold on this part of town, and desperation always had the potential to become danger.

"This is it?" Derby asked, brushing his hands off on his hoodie and looking around the empty rectangular space.

"Not exactly." Doc led the way across the room. There was debris strewn all around the floor, dirt crunched under their boots as they navigated their way to the back corner. Derby had managed to get a little sleep last night, which had taken the edge off, enough for him to function at least, but a portion of his attention was still constantly drawn to the brik in his pocket. A dwindling fuse that could burn out at any moment.

In the corner of the room there were a few stacks of thin metal plates. "Gimme a hand with this." Doc got in position to lift one end of a rather large sheet and Derby joined. As they lifted one side of the plate, a section of the floor underneath came up with it. A mechanism clicked and they let go. The thin metal slab was fixed to the top of a trapdoor which was now latched open before them, the sharp panel jutting out at an angle just above their heads. Doc disappeared down the ladder and through the hatch first. "Come down!" she called up when she reached the bottom.

It was a short climb down the ladder and when he reached solid ground, he heard a *CLICK* behind him and the whole room lit up. They were standing in a surprisingly high-ceilinged, circular space that was filled with an assortment of shabby furniture. The major fixtures of the room were a large, battered dining table that stood in the center, an L-shaped sofa off to the side that looked worse for wear, and an old wooden cabinet with a yellow front panel that sat in the back corner. The space was lit by several strings of warm bulbs that hung across the ceiling. Doc spread her arms out walking to the center of the room "Welcome to the original home of the Bad Moon Crew. Before we got all fancy and moved into something with plumbing."

Derby looked around the room, impressed by how cozy it felt for what was effectively a hole in the ground. "How long did you all live here for?" he asked.

"We moved to the apartment a few years after Marv and I joined up." Doc walked to the back of the hovel, stepping over an array of tattered mattresses that were clustered in the corner, and approached the dusty yellow and wood cabinet. Derby hadn't seen anything like it before. The tall piece of furniture had a glass screen inset into the colored panel on the front and simple black letters that formed a strange word across the top. The original purpose of the relic was unclear.

Doc knelt down, working her fingers into a gap in the wood paneling that ran along the bottom of the cabinet, and removed a section of it. She set the thin wooden sheet down next to a pile of empty, dusty backpacks that leaned up against the rear wall of the hideout. Removing this makeshift door revealed a tiny stash inside, containing a collection of odds and ends: some coins, a pair of broken headphones, a couple of books. Doc rummaged through the items, eventually pulling out an expensive-looking gold pocket watch.

"This was my mum's. I'm not sure why I left it here." She sat down with her back against the wall next to the strange furniture, holding the watch up by its chain, letting it rock back and forth in front of her. "Maybe it was my way of trying to move on." She paused, contemplating. "Just between us, it didn't work," she said with a sad smile.

Derby slid down the wall and sat next to her in the dusty, cobweb ridden corner. "Well shit, if you figure that one out, please, let me know."

Doc laughed. “Will do.” She folded the watch up, letting its chain pool in her hand, and stowed it in her sweater pocket. “For now, this little beauty is gonna help us make Tithe.”

“Really?” Derby asked, looking surprised.

She nodded. “King would *never* ask for it, but this is my way of doing my part I guess.”

“It was your mom’s, though. You’re just gonna. . .give that up?”

Doc shook her head and curled her lips down in a dismissive way. “Nah, it ain’t like that, Sticks. I’m not the sentimental type.” She looked down. “That’s also something I got from mum. Something that I can’t give away.” Her lips curled back up into a smile.

“What about Marv?” Derby asked.

“Oh, he got music. Our parents *loved* music. The blues especially.” She scrunched her nose up in mock disgust. Doc was staring across the room at the ladder that led back up to the decaying structure above, the fingers of her left hand absently tracing the pill shaped tattoo on her right.

“When Marv and I first got here JT was just a little kid, and she *refused* to go to sleep at night unless King was home.” Doc smiled as she remembered. “This was back when King was much more involved in things, so he was out late most nights.” She looked at Derby. “That fancy apartment didn’t come easy.”

She smirked. "Anyway, JT would sit right there." She pointed to the ladder across the room. "Right at the bottom of the ladder, cross-legged on the floor, staring up at the hatch, waiting for him to come home. No matter what Maman tried, the kid held her ground. I'm sure you can imagine; she hasn't changed all that much." Derby laughed. "So, after we'd been here a few months Marv started giving her his music at night. He'd walk right over and put the headphones on her while she was sitting there. I guess he figured it was better than the silence. After a few weeks she started falling asleep curled up under the hatch, music still blaring. King would carry her back to bed when he came home. Then, one night, we'd all been asleep for a while, I turn over and holy shit, there's JT, curled up in her bed, headphones on, fast asleep. King was still out. She never sat under the ladder again."

She smiled. "I've always thought that that was our parents somehow. Living on through Marv, helping that little girl get to sleep." A spell of silence washed over the room and the two Bad Moons sat in it comfortably. For just a moment, the weight of the device in Derby's pocket and all the consequence that came with it, was absent from his mind. Doc started. "It's a bit silly, I—"

"It's not silly at all," Derby said.

Doc nodded. After a few more moments they stood, brushed themselves off, replaced the wooden panel that concealed the stash, turned out the lights and climbed the ladder, leaving the now defunct Bad Moon hideout behind them.

They exited the building back out onto the streets of the southern Reeds, pulling the heavy door closed behind them. Derby gave it an extra tug to make sure it was shut tight, and when he turned around, Doc had her hands up.

The man holding the gun looked scared. He was a wisp of a man dressed in dirty clothes, with burn scars that marred the left side of his face. "Pockets." The word shook in his throat just like the gun in his bony hands.

Doc began calmly. "Listen, we can—"

"Empty your pockets!" The man raised his shaky voice now, not in anger, but in desperation. Derby pulled a few coins that he had in his jacket pocket and tossed them on the ground between them and the man, hoping that would be enough to satisfy him. The man knelt and frantically picked up the coins, all the while keeping his eyes and the pistol trained on the two of them. "You!" he said, gesturing the gun aggressively toward Doc. She turned her empty pants pockets inside out. The man's eyes darted around the deserted street, approaching Doc slowly until the barrel of his pistol was in contact with her chest. The skeletal fingers of the man's free hand wormed their way inside the front pouch of Doc's hoodie and pulled out the gold pocket watch.

The pressure of the gun on Doc's torso caused her hoodie to ride up enough to reveal one of the twin pistols holstered at her side. The sight of the firearm spooked the man, and he jumped back to a distance, gun still aimed at Doc, her mother's watch still in his hand. His fear intensified and his pace quickened as he backed away, reaching the end of the lane, and finally disappearing into a sprint down the cross-street. As soon as the man's gun no longer had her marked, Doc ran to the corner where he had disappeared. Derby followed and when they got to the cross-street there was a crowd of people in the direction the man had fled.

"Dammit!" Doc hit the brick wall of a nearby building. She put her hood up and began to walk back down the street. "Let's just go."

"Aren't we gonna go after—"

"It ain't worth it, Sticks. Trust me."

They made their way back up through The Reeds in silence, crossing the Kin Line, and moving into the city center. A strong feeling of guilt began to well up in Derby as he wondered if he could have done more to help. "I'm really sorry, Doc. I should have—"

"What? Got yourself shot?" She inhaled deep through her

nose. "It's all good, nothing you coulda done," she said without looking back. "Just. . .keep it between us yeah?" Doc lit up a smoke and they forged ahead, disappearing into the noisy turbulence of The Drum.

"Why don't you put your money where your mouth is then?"

JT was on the verge of victory in a redemptive game of eight ball with Marv that Derby was spectating. Doc had chosen to distract herself from what happened earlier by volunteering to help King fix a leak under the kitchen sink while Marisha supervised.

"Nah, see, there's no way to verify it, cher," Marv replied as he just barely missed a shot.

JT scoffed. "We could just ask him."

Marv laughed. "I wouldn't recommend asking the leader of The Black Ashes if he faked having cancer."

"I didn't say he faked it!" JT said, hitting a blue colored ball at a sharp angle and sinking it in a pocket. "I'm saying I think that black cigarette cured him."

"Right, but that doesn't make *any* sense, JT," Marv said, "so, what he's going to hear is: Are you *sure* you had cancer?"

The young girl rolled her eyes. "The thing never goes out, Marv."

"So that means it cured him?"

Derby interjected. "What do you mean it never goes out?"

"I *mean* it never goes out," JT shrugged. "Never burns down, stays lit all the time. Least that's what the Ashes say. I call it 'The Eternal Smoke'," she said proudly, scanning the table for her next shot.

"It's a gimmick," Marv said, hunching over JT as she lined up her cue. "A novelty, designed to do exactly this. To make us talk about it. To build a sense of intrigue around the man." The young girl shooed him away. "But I'll tell you what, if you ever have the balls to get the answer, straight from Jeph, I'll put two coins on it."

"You're on," JT said and fired, this time a red ball disappeared down the hole in the corner of the table. "Ohhh, it's so over!"

Derby smiled absently. Since they returned to the apartment, anxiousness had crept back into his mind. It had been almost twenty-four hours since his encounter with Ruse Gamble, and still, the device in his pocket lay dormant. And still, he was unsure what he would do when it awoke.

"Ay, there we go, someone's been practicing," Marv said with a grin.

JT knocked yet another ball into another pocket. "It's like you said before, focus on what I can do better. Turns out this game's pretty easy." She walked around the table with a confident swagger to line up her final shot.

Marv was still smiling. "You did great, kid. I got one more tip for ya."

JT was carefully lining up the game-winning shot. "Thanks Marv, but I don't think I need it." She called the pocket and struck the white ball but just before it contacted the black one, Marv swiped the eight ball off the table. "Hey! What are you doing?"

The Soulman put the stolen ball in his pocket. "I win."

"You can't do that, that's against the rules!"

"Ah, and that's your next tip cher: The game is rigged against you. Always. You want to win? Make your *own* rules."

"Says who?"

He held the eight ball up close to her face. "Says the guy with the ball."

JT jumped over the table trying to snatch the black orb from his hand and when he pulled it away, she proceeded to chase him around the room trying to wrestle it back from him.

BUZZ. BUZZ.

Derby's heart sank into the floor and his hand shot to

his pocket. It was the brik. He scanned the room nervously, it looked as though no one had noticed anything. Marv and JT were still fighting over the eight ball while the rest of the crew was mulling around the sink in the kitchen. He slunk out of the room, down the hallway to the last bedroom on the right and shut the door behind him. Pulling the device out of his pocket, hands covered in a film of cold sweat, he flipped it open, the screen lighting up his face, the message clear in the small window.

> **TONIGHT. MIDNIGHT. SILVER & SEVENTH. NORTH REEDS.**
> **ALONE.**

5
A SHAPE THAT SERVES US

THIRTY YEARS AGO

"**AHA!** Here it is. Freedom."

The two boys stood in a deserted alleyway in the northern Reeds. A thick-barred grate had been shifted aside, revealing the mouth of a small canal that penetrated one of the tall brick walls bordering the narrow lane. "Freedom? Kinda looks like a dirty tunnel."

"C'mon, Obo," the taller boy said, patting his friend on the back, "use your imagination for once." He crouched down and led the way into the cramped passage. Obo followed, sliding the grate back into place across the entrance, closing the way behind them.

The tunnel was damp and dark; a layer of moisture covered the cold stone. The boys flicked their lighters to life, using the sparks of light to guide them further down the path.

"How did you find out about this anyway?" Obo asked.

The taller boy looked back with mischief in his bright, blue eyes, softly illuminated by the tiny flame of his lighter. "My dad don't talk as quiet as he thinks he does when he has company."

"So, you were eavesdropping."

"Sure, technically, but the ends justify the means." They were deeper into the tunnel now; the walls were starting to widen. "Think about it, Obo. How many hours do we spend at The Hollow doing chores while the old man does his business stuff?"

Obo stopped suddenly. "Cain?"

The taller boy continued. "Imagine we could come and go as we please with my pops none the wiser. When I say freedom—"

"Cain!" Obo raised his lighter, dimly revealing an alcove branching off the tunnel to their left.

Cain walked over, adding his light to the scene, bringing

into view the bottom rungs of a wooden ladder that sprouted up into the darkness. Cain smiled. "*That's* what I mean."

Once the boys reached the base of the ladder they could stand up straight again. Looking up, they could see a small, distorted circle of light where the ladder broke out into the world, some twenty feet above where they were standing. The distance was difficult to gauge. Obo ascended the ladder first, going slow to make sure the wood was still sturdy enough to hold their weight. The ladder creaked and moaned as they carefully climbed, the circle of light growing above them, until they finally reached the top.

Here, at the end of the ladder was another grate, just like the one that had blocked the entrance to the tunnel below them. Obo grabbed one of the thick bars, leaving one hand to balance himself on the wooden rungs, and tried to push the cover free. It wouldn't budge, and the ladder groaned loudly. "Shit. It's stuck."

"Use both hands," Cain instructed from a foot or so below. Obo grabbed the grate in two places and pushed up again hard, the seal around the perimeter of the cover gave out a bit but the ladder protested with a sickening creak. "The ladder is gonna give if I—"

"The ladder will be fine, Obo. You've almost got it."

One more time he grabbed the grate and heaved, this time starting with a twist, and the steel cover came free. Obo slid the grate to the side above him and emerged in the center of a tiled room. The walls around the small area were lined with stacks of boxes filled with fresh fruits, cured meats, and other foodstuffs. Obo was standing in the pantry of The Hollow. "Damn, you were right, Cain. We're–" *CRACK.*

"AH!" As Cain was climbing the last few rungs of the ladder behind his friend, the wood finally gave in to the stress and the ladder collapsed. Obo turned, just in time to see the older boy beginning an involuntary descent back down the hole, and he dove forward catching his friend's hand. Cain was tall but quite thin, and Obo had always been very strong for his age. He heaved, pulling Cain up high enough that he could throw his elbows out onto the tiled floor of the room, then he grabbed the boy by the belt and pulled him the rest of the way up. Cain sprawled out on his back in the middle of the floor, both boys breathing heavily.

"I *told* you the ladder was gonna give!" Obo shouted.

Cain was laughing through his heavy breaths. "Relax, we're good. We'll need to get a new ladder though." Obo cracked a smile and shook his head helping his friend to his feet. "Thank you, brother." Cain said sincerely. The boys put the grate back in its place covering the path to the sewers below and exited the room. The doorway spat them out behind the service counter of an empty diner.

The tall white ceramic surface kept the peace between the

tiny kitchen on one side, and the spacious seating area on the other. Cain hoisted himself up and sat on top of the counter. "This place has belonged to the Gamble family for generations." He looked around the room as if he didn't know The Hollow inside and out. "I wonder how many of 'em knew about the secret we just discovered." His gaze found its way back to Obo. "I say we cut the world outta this one from here forward, keep this between us."

Cain extended his hand; Obo nodded and shook it, cementing an agreement between friends that would stand the test of time.

FIVE YEARS AGO

The Hollow was somewhat of a landmark in the north end of Reed City. The brilliant pink of the neon sign served as an orienting fixture in the area. A long-standing asset of the Gamble family, the diner had always flickered between serving the public and private use for Gamble business. These days, however, its function skewed heavily to the latter. On this particular day, the dining area of The Hollow was full of Gambles and Bad Moons.

DING. A small bell rang out, signaling the opening of the door as the last members of the group entered the restaurant.

The room was filled with the low hum of casual chatter between those gathered. Cain Gamble sat at a table near the center with his back to the door. Behind him, spread out across the various chairs, tables, and booths was a small band of Gamble associates. Among this group were both younger Gamble siblings: Ruse and Natalia; the family's man and Natalia's minder: Simmons; and on Cain's flank, as always, perched his loyal bodyguard, Arthur Rook.

Seated directly across from the Gamble leader was Obo, with The Bad Moon Crew spread out in a similar fashion behind him. The Taylor twins were seated on a table just behind King, with chairs supporting their feet, while Marisha sat on a tall stool at the counter.

"JT." She called out to the young girl who was hovering around the center table, standing informally close to Arthur Rook.

"I turned double digits last week," JT said to the man. Arthur was silent. The boisterous child started to shadowbox with the man's leg. "I think I could take ya." She stopped and looked up at the stoic bodyguard who seemed to pay her no mind at all, staring straight ahead, indifferently. "Why do you always look so mean?" Cain, seated nearby, running his fingers through his big, bushy beard, mostly stifled a grin, but it managed to sneak out through his eyes.

"JT!" The girl hopped back to Marisha and jumped up

onto the stool next to her at the counter. The chatter among the group died down and the room got quiet.

Finally, Cain spoke. "Let's get down to it then. What the *hell* were you two thinking?"

An awkward stillness hung in the air for a moment, then Marv answered. "I got some bad info. Thought the place was gonna be empty. Figured the A's wouldn't even notice anything was missing. Got sloppy, got spotted. So, I guess I wasn't, ay. Thinking, that is. But it was my idea, Nat didn—"

"Got spotted alright, in a Gamble van too." Cain turned. "How 'bout you Natalia? Anything to add?"

Natalia shifted in her booth. "I took the van, it was my plan, Marv was just going along with—"

Cain waved them off exasperatedly. "Cut it out with the hero shit, both of you. You two stole materials from an Uppers facility, got seen doing it in one of *my* vans, and now I've got these pricks knockin' on my door demanding restitution in *triple.* Three hundred and fifty coin." He paused for a moment and took a deep breath. "Obo, thoughts?"

King looked back at Marv sternly. "Ay, a *significant* lapse in judgement, no doubt." The big man ran his hands through his hair. "The Bad Moons will cover the coin. We don't have it all right now, but we'll get it. Or, if you'd prefer, we can work some of it off."

Cain nodded and considered a moment before replying. "One seventy-five. We'll pay the rest. Work off whatever you need to."

Ruse protested immediately. "Cain, that's ridiculous."

"Our sister was just as much a part of this mess. We'll take responsibility for that," the eldest Gamble sibling said sternly.

"She's a Gamble!" Ruse shouted.

Natalia spoke up. "I don't need your protecti—"

Cain turned to his younger siblings. "Enough! Both of you!" The silence that fell over the room was complete. "That's right, Ruse, she's a Gamble. She should damn well know better! As should you." Cain turned back to the Bad Moons to resume the discussion.

Through gritted teeth, Ruse squeaked out a final dissent. "If this was *any* other crew, they wouldn't be walking out of here without paying up. *In full.*"

Cain closed his eyes and breathed through his nose. "Well, this *isn't* any other crew, Ruse. It's The Bad Moon Crew. And whether you like it or not they are an extension of this family." He turned to his younger brother with a look that dared him to speak up again. The younger Gamble remained silent but shot up from his seat and stormed out of the diner, the slamming of the door behind him was punctuated by the pointed sound of the bell.

"Cain, we can pay the three-fifty," Obo said calmly, after a moment.

"Stop, Obo. I've made my decision." Cain dropped his head into his hand, massaging his temples and smoothing down his tightly slicked back hair. He looked tired. "It's getting tougher," he said looking across the table at his friend. It was almost an appeal.

Obo nodded empathetically. "Yeah."

Cain stood. "Well. We'll see you all tomorrow for Feast." Everyone else followed suit and the groups began to file out of the establishment. On the way out, Cain turned and pointed at Marv. "And I want The Soulman here at the break of dawn, ready to cook," he said with a wink. The door closed behind the last person to leave, and the little bell rang throughout the empty interior of The Hollow.

FOUR MONTHS AGO

Rain was coming down hard on The Reeds. The impact of the drops like pebbles on the roof of The Hollow, echoing loudly through the dining area. The only two occupants of the room sat across from each other at the center table, each with a steaming cup in front of them.

"I hear you've taken on a new member," Cain croaked. His voice sounded strained.

Obo nodded. "Ay, good kid. Really been through it, as we all have."

"So, why this one? You've had some kids pass through, but it's been a good while since you've officially adopted a Bad Moon."

The big man shook his head. "I don't well know, to be honest." He paused. "Risking a bit of narcissism, I guess I see a shade of myself in the boy." He noticed that Cain's gaze had wandered. His eyes had dimmed from their usual vibrant blue. "Are you okay, brother?" Like the world outside, the leader of the Gambles was grey, his usual air of solidity replaced by an uncertain wobble, as though wracked by a storm himself.

"Hm?" He cleared his throat. "I'm not sure, Obo."

"I know things are tough. We all feel it. But every year we get—"

"What if we could break it?" Cain's full attention was now on his friend who sat across from him.

"Break what?" Obo asked with a furrowed brow.

"All of it. Take it all apart and put it back together. Piece by piece. Into a shape that serves *us*." There was a slightly manic glint in his eye.

Obo chuckled dismissively, blowing away the steam coming off his cup of coffee before taking a sip. "Sounds like a dream."

"Or a gift." Cain was wide-eyed. "Freedom, Obo. The real thing. Not just a tunnel under a building."

The Bad Moon King considered his friend's words. "I would ask what the price is."

Cain shook his head. "No price. A gift."

"Bullshit. Anybody that can give something like that is extracting a price somewhere. In full and plus some." Obo looked across the table, fixing Cain with a stringent stare. "Nah, brother. Nothing free about any of that from where I'm sittin."

Cain sat back in his chair and let out a deep sigh. The two men sat still, soaking in the greyness of the room for a few minutes.

"I wonder how much of our prison is pursuit," Obo said leaning forward. "What you're talking about is power. We don't have a lot down here, but we've *got* that brother. I feel it every time I walk through The Drum. We used to know it, and then we buried it. In favor of. . .reckless ambition." He sat back in his chair and ran his hands through his hair. "Now it's trapped down below somewhere, *real* power, and it can't get out. We're squeezing so damn tight." He paused. "Maybe we just need to get outta the way."

Cain laughed. "Hah, my friend." He reached across the table, firmly patting Obo on the shoulder. "All these years, and you're *still* pulling me up that ladder." They both smiled.

"I wanna meet the new kid," Cain said, and the two friends continued their conversation in the dining room of The Hollow, until the grey outside turned to black and the only light to guide them as they left the establishment was the blazing pink glow of the sign.

6
HIS CONTEMPTIBLE FRIENDS

THE CORNER OF SILVER and Seventh was deep in the northwestern corner of The Reeds, just on the edge of Gamble territory, and tonight, it was busy. The building that Derby stood in front of was alive, both inside and out. The brickwork walls had been dyed a deep purple which would have been difficult to see in the midnight dark, if not for the blue lights illuminating the structure. The congregation that was gathered inside the establishment had spilled out onto the street, and Derby found himself standing among a small crowd. A glance at his watch told him it was a few minutes after twelve.

He considered heading back to the apartment. It was

cold, and there was no sign of Ruse, Arthur Rook or any other Gamble he recognized. He was tempted to pull the brik from his pocket to confirm he was at the right intersection, but a device like that would most certainly draw attention from someone on the congested sidewalk. Just as he became almost restless enough to begin the journey back to the Bad Moon house, he saw Arthur leaning against the vibrant walls of the building, basking in the soft blue of the lights, the orange glow from his cigarette bouncing off the scarred skin across his eye.

As Derby approached, the man reached into his long jacket and pulled out an envelope, handing it to him when he got close. Rook puffed on his smoke while Derby opened the envelope and discreetly examined the contents. A very used-looking access card fell into his hand along with a small note:

465 PARK STREET

RECORDS, STAFF, DANNY CAHILL

He'd be able to find the address easily enough, but he had many questions about the rest. By the time he looked up from the note Arthur Rook was already far down the street, almost to the other side of the crowd that was concentrated on the corner. Derby called after him hoping to get some clarity, but the man continued his leave, undisturbed. Not wanting to cause a scene or draw any attention to himself, Derby folded the envelope back up with the items inside and tucked it into his jacket pocket. Pulling up his hood, he moved through the crowd in the opposite direction that Arthur had gone, leaving behind the lively establishment at Silver and Seventh. He headed west toward Park Street, where he would locate unit 465 and hope that there, things would become clearer.

His destination was not difficult to find. 465 was a large, flat structure that stood sentry on the elbow at the end of Park Street. Even in the dimness of the late hour, Derby could clearly make out the enormous **A** that decorated the side of the building. This was an Uppers facility.

He found himself seriously weighing all his options from the vantage where he stood, across the street from his target. Burgling an Uppers office was a severe violation and not something that Derby O'Malley was cut out for, even with his limited experience as a Bad Moon these past few months. Would the Gambles come after him if he bailed? If he jumped ship now, he couldn't imagine a way in which he would get another chance to leave The Reeds. As he steered through these waves of doubt, he was softly startled back into the moment by the buzzing of the brik. He pulled the device from his pocket, scanning the area to make sure he was still alone, and flipped it open.

3AM. Drop-Off. Silver & Seventh.

Three o'clock. The walk up Park Street had taken about thirty minutes, which gave him two and a half hours to work with. He was once again roused by the ascending sound of a roaming group of nightlifers coming up the street from the south. His legs moved before his mind could, and he crossed the road, tugging his hood further over his sandy hair, and briskly entering the shadow of the structure that was his assignment.

Derby rounded the corner to the rear of the facility, finding safety from the eyes of the passing group. A narrow dirt road wound through the large lot behind the building, snaking all the way up to a wide bay door. Next to this large entrance was a short set of steps leading up to a smaller one. He made his way across the rocky path and up the steps, his head on a swivel the whole way, but the building was quiet. Reaching the door, he found a panel mounted beside the frame. Removing the envelope from his jacket, he dug out the worn-looking access card, and after a moment of hesitation, scanned it.

BEEP. A green light at the top of the panel lit up, and the door clicked loudly. He pushed the door open just enough that he could slip through the gap, letting it close behind him.

The room that welcomed him on the inside was a sprawling warehouse floor lined with many tall racks, each stocked full of pallets and crates of all sizes. Derby immediately noticed two things upon entering. Firstly, that it was very warm; not something typical of any location in The Reeds, inside or out, at this time of year. And second, he noticed that the crates stashed on the shelves were identical to the one he and the Taylor twins had pilfered a few nights ago down in the south side. The first letter of the name **AUGUSTA**, that was stenciled on the side of the wooden boxes, exactly matched the giant one painted on the outside of the building.

There was nobody in this room as best as he could tell from a quick scan, but he noticed a doorway leading off to the right. With no clear direction, other than the note in his jacket, he made his way across the warehouse and slunk out of the room, pressing deeper into the facility.

Much like the last room, the hallway was warm and well-lit. After a short trip, he came to a point where the path fractured in a few directions. An assortment of signs hung from the ceiling at this juncture, each one an arrow that named a destination and suggested a direction to get there. One of the signs pointed back up the hallway, the way Derby had come from, and read **INVENTORY/RECEIVING**. **ACCOUNTING** pointed off down a passage to the left, and finally, pointing straight ahead, were two signs, one that read **FRONT DESK** and another that read **RECORDS**.

Derby rustled the envelope out of his jacket and slid out the note.

RECORDS, STAFF, DANNY CAHILL

It seemed his objective was straight ahead, so he continued. The corridor came to an end after a while, culminating in an elbow in the hall. As he approached the corner, Derby could hear what sounded like voices from around the bend, so he slowed down. Once he reached the corner, he was able to identify the sound: it was the jagged noise of the Reed City news broadcast.

Quietly, he peeked around the corner and found, on the other side of a short passage, the welcome room of the facility. In the center of the large rotunda was a heavy desk that faced down the front entrance leading out to Park Street. The man seated at the desk looked far too comfortable to be much of a guard; feet kicked up, absorbed in the glow of a screen which was the source of all the sound. The room was filled with the drone of a man on the broadcast discussing the completion of construction in The Drum.

Aside from the main entrance, there were only three paths off the large foyer: a door behind the front desk with a small restroom badge on the wall beside it, the hallway that Derby was crouched in, and, directly opposite this, another hallway that was cut short by a door. A door with a sign above it that read **RECORDS**.

Where he needed to go was clear, but the way there was complicated by the doorman at the desk. Right then, as though his thoughts had spurred the universe into action, the guard stood up from his post, stretching and heading into the restroom behind the desk.

As soon as the door closed behind the man, Derby quickly and quietly crept across the rotunda. He crossed in front of the desk, being careful to step over a tangle of cables that were clumsily gathered around a small cutout in the heavy piece of furniture. Derby paused when he reached the far end of the desk, double checking on the restroom door before continuing. When he reached the short hallway on the other side, he took one final look back, making sure the guard was still preoccupied, and then proceeded to the marked door. He found another panel here, identical to the one that permitted him into the facility, and once again the card in the envelope made the panel glow green, and the door click open. Derby stepped slowly into the records room making sure the door shut softly behind him.

The room was a veritable labyrinth of filing cabinets; short, tall, wide, and narrow. The spaces between them were just barely large enough for a person to open the drawers and browse the contents. It was dimmer in here than the rest of the facility he'd seen so far, but he was still able to make out the section plates at the end of each row. He walked past **MAINTENANCE**, **PERMITS** and **SECURITY** before stopping at **STAFF**. It looked like it spanned about five aisles, the largest section in the room. Checking his watch put the time at just past one o'clock. He started down the first aisle and got to work.

The files were organized by last name so finding **CAHILL, DANNY** shouldn't have been difficult, except that the records were divided into subsections by company. Having no idea where Danny worked, he decided to run through all the **C** files from company to company. Mr. Cahill was nowhere to be found among the ranks of the Augusta Rail Service, nor was he in the employ of Summit Healthcare. Due to their weight, the drawers of the file cabinets threatened to screech loudly while being opened or shut, so Derby had to be very careful during his search to limit the noise he made. He rifled through what felt like at least fifty company rosters, until he finally found Danny.

Under the subsection labelled **REED CITY HYDRO**, was the file he had been sent to collect.

CAHILL, DANNY. DIRECTOR OF OPERATIONS.

There was an image of the man at the top of the first page, Derby didn't recognize him. But this must have been what he was here for. While browsing the file, he caught sight of his wrist and noticed it was two o'clock. He had spent almost an hour in the records room and had only one hour left to get back uptown and meet Arthur. Snapping the file closed and shutting the heavy drawer, he crept quickly back to the entrance.

Derby snuck out of the records room and back into the short hallway as quietly as he could, making his way far enough down the passage that he could peek out and see the guard's desk which was, at the moment, empty. The soundscape of the room was still dominated by the thin voices coming from the monitor on the desk. He peeked out into the room fully; the man was nowhere to be seen. The uncertainty of the guard's absence was more unnerving than the danger of his presence.

Throwing caution to the wind, Derby began inching his way across the rotunda. He considered leaving through the main entrance, but Park Ave got busy, even this late into the night, and the last thing he wanted was to be spotted fleeing an Uppers facility.

As Derby approached the empty desk in the center of the room, thudding footsteps echoed from the hallway that led back to the warehouse, the steps gradually poking through the noise of the television, announcing someone's approach. After looking frantically around the empty room, Derby was left with the only thing he could think of. He tucked himself behind the rope of cables, into the cutout under the desk. From this spot, he couldn't see much of anything. The thick wood of the furniture separated him from the sitting side of the desk, which is where the footsteps came to a halt.

Derby swallowed his heartbeat and directed all the air bound for his lungs through his nose, trying to remain as silent as possible. The guard stood near his chair without taking a seat and sipped something loudly. After hovering there for another moment, the man thudded his way off once more, footsteps echoing toward the records room. They continued in that direction and eventually Derby heard the familiar beep and click of the access panel, followed by the door opening. Very slowly, he poked his head out from the hiding spot under the desk, finding the door to the records room wide open, and the guard nowhere in sight. Seizing the opportunity, he crawled out from the tiny nook and darted toward the opposite corridor.

In his haste, he tripped on the nest of cables that were coiled on the floor in front of the desk and fell hard, dropping the Cahill file, and pulling one of the power cords out from its socket. Regrettably, the cable that came loose was the one giving life to the noisy monitor. The abrupt shift from the full volume of the broadcast to the vacuum of nothing was so jarring that the resultant silence was deafening.

In a frenzied panic, Derby snatched up the Cahill file, jumped to his feet and ran, as fast as he could. He didn't look back to see if the man was in pursuit, or if he had even noticed the commotion. He just ran. Up the hallway, through the big warehouse past the tall racks of crates, and out the door to the lot behind the facility. Derby didn't slow down when he hit open air, he kept running across the dusty road and back onto Park Street, not once looking back.

His pace slowed to a brisk walk once he was a few blocks away from the facility. The streets were mostly quiet, but after he had worked off a bit of the panic, Derby became at once conscious of drawing attention to himself. The rest of the way back to Silver and Seventh was a dizzy blur of anxiety and adrenaline.

He arrived at the intersection, just as three o'clock struck, the crowd he had escaped from a few hours prior on the stoop of the purple-bricked establishment had vanished. The absence of the mob made the striking shape of Arthur Rook somehow more intimidating; a crooked figure waiting on the corner, illuminated from behind by the moody, blue glow of the empty club. Derby briskly approached and handed the Gamble enforcer the stolen file.

While the man skimmed the contents, Derby managed to stammer out a string of words describing how he was pretty sure he hadn't been seen, that there *was* a close call, but it probably wasn't a big deal. If Arthur paid mind to any of what the young man was saying, his face didn't show it. Satisfied with the file and tucking it into his long jacket, Rook held out his hand expectantly. It took a second, but Derby eventually clued in and handed back the envelope containing the access card and the note. Arthur pocketed this as well, but his hand remained outstretched, waiting for more. It took longer this time, but after a few moments of staring blankly at the scarred man, Derby reached into his pocket and pulled out the brik. Relinquishing the device felt like giving away the last piece of proof he had to himself that this transaction ever occurred. Arthur took the brik and swiftly hid it away with the other items in the folds of his coat.

Another salad of words fell out of Derby's mouth; he asked about where to go from here, and how to contact Ruse. The man stated simply that they would be in touch and promptly walked away, disappearing down Silver Avenue, into the dead of night.

The journey back to the Bad Moon apartment was quiet. When Derby finally made it home and fumbled his way into bed, he lay awake for a long time. There was a heaviness in his gut. Like he had swallowed concrete, and it had begun to set around his insides. It was a wrong feeling. One he wished he had felt sooner.

When Derby awoke the next morning, he wasn't sure if he had slept at all. Rather than lay there and continue to wrestle with consciousness, he decided to get up. Bleary-eyed, he made his way to the kitchen.

JT was the only other Bad Moon awake. The young girl gave him a nod as he passed her where she sat on the pool table, inches from the television, watching the news. He said good morning, but her headphones blocked it out.

Derby grabbed a cup, filled it with water and headed out onto the balcony, closing the door behind him. Looking out across Reed City in the morning sun, he tried to let his mind wander, but it chose to stay firmly planted on the events of the previous evening. He wondered if and how Ruse would reach out to him and what his plan was for helping Derby get out of The Reeds. Would the man hold up his end of the deal? The heavy, concrete feeling was creeping back into his center, if it had left at all.

"*PARK STREET LAST NIGHT—*"

Derby jumped. The television in the house was blaring so loud he could hear it clear through the door. He hurried back inside and found JT standing on the table, looking at him wild-eyed, holding the dangling cord of her unplugged headphones.

"*AGAIN, THAT'S ONE DERBY O'MALLEY WHO IS WANTED BY THE AUGUSTA AUTHORITIES FOR THE THEFT OF SENSITIVE MATERIALS FROM A SECURE FACILITY IN THE EARLY HOURS OF THIS MORNING. MR. O'MALLEY'S WHEREABOUTS ARE NOT KNOWN AT THE MOMENT, BUT WE HAVE RECEIVED WORD THAT HE IS CLOSELY ASSOCIATED WITH THE LOCAL GROUP: 'THE BAD MOON CREW'. IF ANYBODY HAS ANY INFORMATION ON MR. O'MALLEY OR HIS CONTEMPTIBLE FRIENDS, PLEASE CONTACT US AT—*"

The concrete in Derby's stomach turned to lead, burning a hole through him, and his world suddenly shrank.

JT, breathing heavy through the shock, unleashed. "WHAT THE F—"

7
ON THE PATH OF MY AMBITION

"—FUCK!"

The roar of the television, punctuated by JT's shriek, had awoken the house and the rest of the Bad Moon Crew were filing out of their bedrooms. Derby was rooted to the floor, not so much in fear, but in despair. It seemed the group had understood the broad strokes of the situation through the walls; they looked at him now with a mix of confusion and accusation. King picked up the remote and lowered the volume of the voices that spilled from the screen. He fixed Derby with a serious stare and spoke in a measured tone. "Sticks, I need you to tell me everything, the full truth, right now."

Derby sunk into one of the chairs around the dining table,

feeling the complete lowness of the moment, and found he had no desire to be anything other than honest, so he told them all of it. He told them about Ruse's proposition in the alley, about meeting up with Arthur in the north side, and all the details of his incursion into the Park Street facility, including the close call on his way out. When the story was done, the horrible lowness remained, but the weight of the secret was lifted at least.

King paced back and forth listening to Derby's confession and when he finished, the big man let out an exasperated noise. "Jesus. . ." He looked at the temporary Bad Moon with confused disappointment. "Why wouldn't you come to me?"

"Ruse said if I told *anyone* the whole thing would be off," Derby replied, his head in his hands. "I thought if it went to shit, it would be *my* problem. I didn't think you'd all get dragged into it."

"Hell, you *really* didn't think," Doc chimed in. Derby looked up and met the girl's eyes, behind a surface layer of steel he could see genuine hurt, and this caused him to sink lower still. "This isn't just some lifted supplies that we can give back, Sticks. This was. . .I mean fuck, you don't even know *what* this was. Some goddamn files? Files that, oh yeah, we don't even *have* anymore. So, returning what you stole and trying to grovel our way out of this is off the table."

"Okay. Alright," King said, gesturing for calm. "We'll

figure this out."

"It doesn't have to be *we*." Derby stood. "They're only looking for me, right? So, I turn myself in and keep you all out of it."

JT folded her arms. "*I'm* not stoppin' ya."

"No," King asserted. "You ain't doin' that Sticks. We can sort this out. I'll talk to Ruse and—"

"No, King. I made the mess, I'll pay the price." Derby walked to the front door of the apartment.

"Sticks," Marisha said sternly, "do you know what that price is?" He turned and looked at them all. "You'll never see the light of day again," she cautioned.

Derby breathed deep. "Yeah, well. . .I've been having trouble with that anyway." He turned back and reached for the doorknob.

BZZT. "*Well, isn't this quite the ordeal.*"

The voice of Ruse Gamble rang out from the HAM radio in the corner of the room. King, with a look of frustration, walked over and picked up the handheld transmitter that was attached to the device. "*Why* Ruse? Why'd you have to drag him into this?"

"*Well, I certainly regret it now. Is the kid there?*"

Derby let go of the doorknob and walked back across the

room. The Bad Moon leader held the transmitter up for him to speak. "I. . .I'm not sure what happened. I guess they saw me. I'm sorry."

"Ruse," King said, "we need to work something out, I won't let Sticks go down for this." He paused for a moment. "Whatever you need."

A long sigh came over the radio. "*The Hollow. Eight o'clock tonight. I'll make sure the A's stay off you until then. Bring the kid.*"

King put down the transmitter and leaned over the table. The room was silent. Derby stared at the floor, avoiding eye contact with anyone else.

Marv spoke first. "Something stinks here, King."

The big man replied without looking up. "Don't get it twisted, Ruse will use this as an opportunity to leverage something from us, no doubt, but he *will* help."

"But why use Sticks in the first place? Why not just send Rook? Or any one of his hundred other minions?" Doc asked, sharing her brother's concern.

"For this reason, exactly." King turned to face the group. "Shit hits the fan, and he's miles away from it. Even better, he gets to step in now, make the mess go away, and extract a prize for that too."

"Or *maybe* Ruse could just smell the stupid on him," JT

jabbed, gesturing to Derby.

"JT," Marisha scolded, "everyone in this room has made mistakes."

"Amen," Marv said.

"Some bigger than others, granted." Marisha gave Derby a stern look. "But mistakes nonetheless," she continued, "and we *always* stand by each other. Ruse Gamble is a son of a bitch that saw an opportunity to take advantage of a kid in pain." She looked back at JT. "Be lucky it wasn't *you* in his crosshairs."

JT scoffed but accepted Marisha's words. Derby sank, once again, into a nearby chair. King walked over and put his hand on the young man's shoulder. "We'll go to The Hollow tonight, and we'll get this sorted. Together."

The brilliant pink of The Hollow's sign poked out over the rooftops like a beacon, helping to guide their way through the streets of the north side. The sun was just beginning to kiss the horizon, setting fire to the sky. So far, Ruse had been true to his word; the A's hadn't come beating down the door looking for Derby, not yet anyway. This did little to quell the group's distrust of the man. Just as the day had done little to temper their aversion toward Derby.

When The Bad Moon Crew reached the sidewalk across from The Hollow, King stopped and gestured for them to do the same. The Taylor twins felt around under their jackets, making sure their weapons were still in place where they had strapped them.

King turned to the group. "Stay alert, but don't let Ruse get a rise out of you in there. Let him showboat a bit, I'm sure he will. We need him right now so just let it roll." He looked around at each member of his crew, as if to assure them individually. "We're gonna get this sorted out," he said, focusing his gaze on his partner. Marisha nodded and the rest of the group followed suit, though Derby wasn't sure.

"I got a real bad feeling," JT said quietly, as if she were reading his thoughts.

King took himself down to her level and put his hand on her shoulder. "We're gonna be fine, little one. Trust me." He tapped the side of her nose and brought himself back to full height. "Now, let's get this over with, ay."

He led them across the street and through the door into the familiar diner.

DING. The group filed into The Hollow and were surprised by how empty it was. Ruse was waiting for them at the usual table in the center of the room, and the only other occupant of the restaurant was Arthur Rook, who sat in a booth near the window.

"Ah, here they are. The Bad Moon Crew." The Gamble leader welcomed them in with a smug smile. More than ever the restaurant reflected its title. An emptiness imbued the room in both space and spirit. Tonight, the place truly was hollow.

King sat in the chair directly across from Ruse and the rest of the Bad Moons found scattered spots among the tables behind him.

"Disappointed?" Ruse asked. King tilted his head slightly. "I'm sure you'd rather be sitting across from my brother."

"Hm." King nodded. "Well, I reckon you'd *also* prefer it to be him."

Ruse smiled.

Derby had taken a spot at a table just beside the one the Taylor twins were sitting on. His eyes nervously wandered to the booth at the back of the restaurant where Arthur Rook was sitting, playing with his sleek knife, twirling it around between his fingers, looking distant through the window at the waning light outside.

"So," Ruse asserted, grabbing Derby's attention back, "where do we go from here?"

King leaned forward. "Come on, Ruse. We know how this goes. Tell us what you need from us and we—"

"Maybe we could start with an explanation from Mr.

O'Malley," Ruse said, sliding his gaze from King over to the table where Derby was sitting.

Derby shifted nervously in his seat. "Uh, sure. Do you want it from the beginning or—"

"Just the part that landed you on the fucking news, son."

Derby found himself on the receiving end of an expectant look from the Gamble leader and he did his best to stammer through a retelling of his escape from the Park Street facility, detailing his trip-and-fall over the nest of cables and his subsequent mad dash out of the place. ". . .and I just kept running. Honestly, I didn't even look back to see if the guard followed. I guess he must have spotted me somehow."

Ruse nodded slowly, considering Derby's story. "You weren't spotted, kid."

Derby's brow furrowed. "I don't really know how else—"

"You know who *was* though?" Ruse wagged his finger at King with a heavy smirk. "One of Jeph's boys. *He* was seen poking his nose around Gamble House."

As Ruse turned back to face King, Derby noticed a faint blue glow just behind the man's left ear.

"How do you know I wasn't spotted?" Derby asked, his breath becoming slightly shallower. Ruse had formed an interrogative eye contact with King that he seemed intent on holding.

"You should talk to Jeph about that," the Bad Moon leader replied, returning Ruse's stare.

"Oh, I did." Ruse sat back but didn't break his gaze with the much bigger man. "He played clueless of course. Besides, turns out the guy we saw doesn't run with the Ashes anymore." He suddenly leaned over the table again with a hunger in his eyes as though he had just won a game and was on the verge of a celebration. "But he *is*, in fact, an old friend of the one and only, 'King' Obo Kalima."

The Gamble leader held his hands open in front of him as though he was presenting King to the room. Derby saw the strange light behind Ruse's ear get a little brighter.

King shook his head. "Ruse, I dunno what you're getting at with this, but can we get back to what we're here for?"

Derby couldn't help himself and cut in again. "Mr. Gamble, how do you know I wasn't—"

"Because I set you up!" Ruse slammed his fist on the table, the previously subtle light behind his ear now blazed blue, no longer a peculiarity only noticed by a keen eye, but a source that illuminated the area around the man. He fixed Derby with an incredulous stare and Derby's body tensed completely, his teeth gnashed together, but he couldn't make a sound, frozen in anger.

"I used you, son." A faint glimmer of pity flashed across Ruse's face. "I used *you* to get to the Bad Moons." He looked around at the rest of the crew, who seemed to be similarly fixed in place by either shock or rage. "Don't be too hard on the kid. This was always gonna be where we ended up, one way or another. Mr. O'Malley was just. . .the path of least resistance."

Ruse stood and began pacing back and forth in front of the table where King sat. "And now, here you are, The Bad Moon Crew. Hunted by the A's, facing serious prosecution, sitting at *my* table, asking me for help." He leaned over the table getting his face close to King's. "I *know* you're scheming something, getting your little friends to creep around Gamble House."

It suddenly registered with Derby that King hadn't moved a muscle since Ruse started his tirade. None of them had.

"That doesn't matter now though."

Ruse returned to his back-and-forth pace, wiping a heavy layer of sweat away from his brow. "In fact, that doesn't even really play into this. This is not about you poking around in my business or getting in my way. You're *not* some necessary, regrettable casualty on the path of my ambition." He stopped in front of King and looked him right in the eye. "I simply don't like you, Obo. I never have." The words were delivered slowly and dripped with pure venom. "That's all this is."

Shocked that the Bad Moons hadn't responded in outrage, Derby tried to turn to the Taylor twins but found he was unable to move his head. In fact, the only part of himself he had control over was his eyes. Looking as far as he could into his peripheral, he found that the others were also subdued, each of them sitting unnaturally still.

"Nothing to say about that, '*King*?'" Ruse said with a sneer. "Oh, that's right, you *can't* say anything." The Gamble leader turned his head, revealing the source of the mysterious, blaring light. In the space behind the man's left ear, at the base of his skull, was a small circular implant grafted onto his skin. If there hadn't been such a bright blue emanating from it, it would've been hard to make out the device.

Ruse tapped on the implant. "New toy." He turned back to the group, wiping a fresh layer of sweat from his forehead. "One that will allow me to usher in an age of freedom for The Reeds."

He gestured to Arthur who jumped up from his booth at the back of the restaurant and made his way to the center of the diner, floating his serrated blade from one finger to the next as he stalked closer. "Unfortunately, you won't be around to see it." Ruse turned his back, facing the entrance of the diner as Arthur approached the table. The scarred man paused for a second, letting the knife settle in his hand, and then unceremoniously sliced a surgical line across King's throat.

Derby summoned every ounce of willpower he could muster, trying desperately to push his body to move, to cry out, to do anything, but he simply could not. Or rather, it felt as though the attempt was never even allowed to begin. King also remained locked in a stone-like position, even as a red waterfall flowed from the line under his chin, soaking the front of his shirt. Arthur tipped King's chair backwards, sending him falling to the floor and turned his attention to Derby, stepping toward him, bloody blade in hand.

"No. Just Obo," Ruse called out. Arthur stopped and pulled out a handkerchief, wiping the knife clean. "We'll let the A's take care of the others." As if on cue, flashing yellow lights flooded the room through the windows of the diner as Ruse and Rook hurried out of The Hollow. *DING.*

The second the door slammed shut behind the Gambles, Derby collapsed to the ground, his equilibrium in shambles. A shaky, yet primal scream from JT broke the unnatural silence, as her and Marisha began stumbling their way over to King. Derby worked his way to his hands and knees, managing to crawl over to the big man, reaching him first.

King lay there, stiff, on his back. Though the color had drained from his skin, his shirt had soaked through with blood, and his wide eyes stared vacantly up at the ceiling, the king of the Bad Moons wore a defiant smile on his face. As if in mockery of the crimson smile across his throat.

END PART ONE

Part Two

Gamble House

8

THE ONLY PLACE LEFT

IT WAS ALL RED. The palm of Derby's shaking hand was painted rose as he removed it from King's damp chest. The pulsing yellow lights that heralded the A's as their vehicles surrounded the building took on a tint from the pink sign of The Hollow and burned through the windows of the diner like fire.

It was all red. And it was all loud. The kind of deafening roar that creates a vacuum of quiet at the center and King's lifeless body was the eye of the storm.

Derby saw the agony on JT's face as she screamed for their fallen leader, pawing at his body, trying to shake him back to life. He watched Marisha take a moment to lament her partner, gently kissing his forehead, and then, after promptly wiping her own tears, begin to settle the young girl next to her.

For Derby this all happened on mute. If these things made noise, his brain didn't register it. He watched Marisha turn to him, saw her lips move as they formed words. Words that looked pressing. As he was trying to work out the shape of what she was saying, someone grabbed his shoulder and yanked him back, out of the eye and into the cyclone of sound.

"STICKS!" Doc's face was streaked with grief, but she managed to maintain an urgency about her. Derby could suddenly feel the sweat on his neck and forehead. And he could hear everything.

"We need to go!" Marisha said to the group, though the words were pointed at JT who was still deeply dismayed. The young girl's sobs and screams were sharp and hurt Derby's ears.

"We can't just walk out the front door, Maman," Marv said.

Marisha pointed behind the counter. "The pantry, in the back."

In his peripheral, Derby could see Marv heading toward the tall counter, but he couldn't take his eyes off King. This was all his fault. No matter what angle he approached it from in his head, *he* was the reason the Bad Moon leader lay there. Cold. Gone. Derby was tugged again as Doc grabbed him by the arm and pulled him along into the bowels of the restaurant.

Marisha spoke softly into JT's ear. "I'm so sorry." She lifted the girl up by the waist, carrying her flailing body behind the counter and into the small room off the dining area, joining the others. And there they left him, Obo 'King' Kalima, on the floor of The Hollow, still smiling and steeped in red.

The pantry was mostly bare; a few short stacks of questionable looking foodstuffs sparsely littered around the room's edge. Marisha entered and put JT down; Marv took over the task of calming the girl. The, now, eldest Bad Moon walked into the middle of the room and knelt, twisting and sliding a heavy grate that sealed the drain in the center of the tiled floor. She motioned urgently for the group to join her. When Derby reached the opening he could see a sturdy, steel ladder descending into the darkness. The Taylor twins went down first, Marisha sent JT down next and then motioned for Derby to follow.

DING. The A's had entered the building.

Marisha briskly followed Derby down and as she entered the hole, she slid the grate back into place above them, all the while keeping her balance on the ladder.

When their feet hit the wet stone passage at the bottom, Doc pulled out her lighter, providing them with a small radius of warm glow. She handed the tiny torch to Marisha, who led them down the damp tunnel, everyone crouching when the passage narrowed enough to warrant it. The youngest Bad

Moon had been soothed to the point that she could function, and she followed the group in silence. In fact, none of them spoke as they navigated the passages below the streets, as if words would make the moment real. Derby couldn't tell if it had been five minutes or twenty, but eventually they reached another grate, this one spat them out into an alleyway several blocks south of The Hollow.

The Bad Moons carefully and quickly made their way south. Five hooded figures moving urgently in the fading light, away from the A's and toward their home. More than ever the streets of The Reeds felt claustrophobic as they weaved through them, doing their best to stick to alleys or crowds. The whole place felt like a maze they were not meant to escape. The bustle and glow of The Drum began to intensify as they got closer to the center of the city. Now, just a few blocks away from the market, they neared the end of a narrow alleyway with Marisha at the head of the group. Just as the woman emerged onto the street, she stopped abruptly.

"Here!" an officer announced loudly from down the street. They had been spotted by a roaming patrol.

Marisha turned back down the alley, and they all ran. Derby could hear the heavy boots of the officers in pursuit behind them as well as the chatter of their radios. The group managed to make some space between them and the A's by weaving from alley to alley, but yellow lights flashed at the end of streets and around corners; many officers were starting to converge on their location.

"We need to split 'em up," Marv said, stopping sharply.

"Marv!" Doc tried to protest.

"Go. They ain't catching me." He winked as he began his ascent up a nearby fire escape. "I'll catch up with you!" he shouted down to them as Marisha hurried the group along.

There were only a few A's that had direct eyes on the Bad Moons, and two of them had now broken off to follow Marv. Marisha turned sharply left leading them down a long stretch and straight into the raging activity of The Drum. Almost immediately they were able to break line of sight from the officers that pursued them and evaporate into the crowd. The group made a beeline through the sea of bodies to the east side of the market, bursting out of the busyness, staying low, and running into Aunt Chel's shop.

The old woman was sweeping the floor behind the counter. "Maman! What are—"

"He's gone, Chel. King's gone. We need to hide," Marisha said, wide-eyed.

The woman looked a little shaken but asked no questions, ushering them behind the counter and into a back room. The five of them squished into the small space, tucking behind boxes where they could, but this was more of a closet than a room. After a few minutes of silence, they heard the door to the shop open and the characteristic heavy footsteps of at least two A's entered. Derby could hear muffled voices through the door.

"Evening officers, I was just closing up." To Derby's surprise, Aunt Chel spoke in a convincingly relaxed voice.

"Chel. The Bad Moon Crew. You see them around tonight?" one of the officers asked sternly.

"Bad Moons? No sir, ain't seen no Bad Moons since yesterday morn'." There was a short, uncomfortable pause. "They in some sorta trouble?"

"Could say that. Mind if we take a look in the back?" The thudding footsteps started around the counter.

"Back here? That's just my stock closet." Nerves began to worm their way into Aunt Chel's voice. The Bad Moons held their breath as the footsteps closed in on the door to their cramped hiding spot.

BZZT. "203, we got eyes on one of them heading toward the east side of The Drum and heading there fast. Backup requested."

The voice had come through the officers' radios, and they stomped into a run, away from the door to the tiny room, and out of the store, without a word. There was a collective sigh of relief before Doc hissed, "That's Marv. They haven't got him yet." She got up. "We should go hel—"

Marisha put her hand out and held back the younger woman, shaking her head. "He'll be okay, Doc. He'll lose them."

Doc nodded hesitantly and sat back down. After what felt like a reasonable amount of time, Marisha got up and very gently opened the door, peeking her head out, then motioned for them to follow.

"Bless you, Chel. I'm so sorry for the trouble," Marisha said, giving the old woman a brief embrace as they walked past her toward the door.

"What do you mean he's gone, Maman? What. . ."

But the Bad Moons were already mostly filed out into the bustling night. "We'll explain later," Doc called back as they exited the homely little shop, leaving Aunt Chel to wonder and worry, with a broom in her hand.

They made it, without incident, a few blocks south to the end of Ellis Ave, where they could see their apartment. Skulking in the shadows of the alley across the street, they were able to spot at least two vehicles belonging to the A's, staked out along the road.

"Fuck!" Doc threw herself back against the brick wall of the alley in frustration. JT kept her head down, staring at the pavement around her feet. The girl had yet to speak a word since they left The Hollow.

Derby had been quiet as well, but the shock was beginning

to dull, just a bit. "What do we do now?" he asked, as much to the world as to the group around him.

Doc spoke, her eyes beginning to glisten. "Marv's still out there and," she gestured to the building across the street, "we can't go home. Where do we go?"

Marisha breathed in deeply, putting her arm around JT and pulling the girl in close to her side. "The only place left."

CREAK. Marisha and Derby opened the heavy steel door as slowly and quietly as they could, trying not to draw any unwanted attention to themselves. They'd had a quiet journey down to the south side, encountering only a few patrols along the way which they'd easily avoided. The efforts of the A's seemed focused in the north of the city, at least for now.

The crew entered the abandoned building and shut themselves inside, carefully fumbling their way across the room to the hidden hatch under the large sheet of metal, not wanting to risk any light.

Once below, Doc flicked the switch, lighting up the hanging strings of warm bulbs overhead as Derby, the last one down the ladder, closed the hatch above him. They stood in silence for a while around the large table at the center of the hovel. As the initial shock began to wear off, all the expected emotions for their situation began to set in: grief, uncertainty, anger.

"Does anyone else know about this place?" Derby asked, his voice thin and hoarse.

Marisha shook her head. "No."

"Do you think Marv will. . ." Doc had a look of deep worry on her face. One that only shows itself when someone you love is in danger. Derby knew this look well.

"He'll find us," Marisha assured her. "This is the first place he'll think to go after the apartment."

JT walked slowly around the table to where Derby was standing and gave him a soft, half-hearted punch in the arm. She hit him again, this time with a little more sting. Then she fell into a rhythm, laying into his arm over and over with decent force, tears flowing freely down her face. It hurt, but Derby didn't recoil or say a word. As her silent tears turned into heavy sobs, her punches weakened, until she hit him with one last, half-hearted shot. The young girl tugged her hood up over her face and walked back to one of the torn-up mattresses on the outskirts of the room, throwing herself onto the thin bedding and curling up into a ball, shaking as she wept.

They looked like hell, standing in the old hideout, and felt it too. Derby's arm was numb where the girl had unleashed her anger. "I'm sor—"

"Don't, Sticks," Doc said, shaking her head. "He used you. The bastard said it himself, he would've found another way."

Derby nodded slowly. "Why?" he asked, a tone of disbelief in his voice. He couldn't understand why someone would intentionally do so much damage to the world around them.

"Because he could?" Marisha suggested. "Cause he's a petulant *shell* of a man?" she spat. ". . .I don't kn—"

Doc held a finger up across her lips and the group fell silent. Derby could very faintly hear some rustling upstairs, not a thing that would've worried him if Doc hadn't brought their attention to it. *CLICK.* They heard the trapdoor at the top of the ladder swing open. Doc and Marisha drew their weapons, the younger woman inching closer to the opening.

"It's me." Marv's whispered voice echoed down into the hideout. The group recognized it right away and holstered their firearms. The older Taylor twin came down the ladder, pulling the hatch closed behind him. Before his feet could even make contact with the ground, Doc had caught him in an embrace, which he happily returned.

"Thank God, you're okay," Doc said.

"You weren't followed?" Marisha asked softly.

Marv shook his head. "Ran 'em way up north and lost 'em there. Stopped by the apartment, clocked the stakeouts, figured this was where y'all would've come." He took a moment to catch his breath. "*Putain*. Maman, what are we—"

"Not now," Marisha said, walking back to the mattress where JT had finally cried herself to sleep. "We should try and get some rest if we can. Clear our heads. We'll talk in the morning."

The Taylor twins nodded wearily and proceeded to the back of the room. Derby headed to the smallest square of bedding in the corner and threw a thin blanket over himself. He felt far from tired and wasn't expecting to sleep at all until his body hit the mattress and the post-adrenaline-dump fatigue pulled him down into a dreamless slumber.

Derby shot upright, pulled harshly from his sleep and into the waking world by the commotion above. The rest of the Bad Moons had also been roused by the noise; Marisha was already stepping delicately toward the exit with her weapon in hand.

They could hear heavy footsteps flooding the room upstairs alongside muffled voices. The words were too quiet for any of them to make out properly, though they sounded frantic. The flurry of thudding boots calmed as the voices rose. Someone had started yelling.

BANG. BANG.

Derby jumped at the gunshots. The breath of everyone in the room quickened. After a tense moment, footsteps fluttered overhead again, punctuated by the dulled creak and clang of the thick door being slammed shut in the room above, followed by a precarious silence.

The crew looked around at each other tentatively, not sure what to do next. They sat in the quiet for a while, until enough time had passed, without further incident, that Marisha deemed it safe to climb the ladder and carefully unlatch the trapdoor, peeking her head out into the upper level. After surveying the room, she brought her face back into view.

"Two of you, come with me," she said, pushing the trap open until it latched, and ascending all the way out of the hideout. Doc got up from her mattress, strapping the belt that carried her twin pistols around her waist, and ran to the ladder. Derby followed.

When they emerged into the room above, they found Marisha crouched over a body in the far corner. The junk-strewn space was quite dim, lit only by the yellow glow of early morning sneaking into the room between the boards that covered the windows. Derby let the hatch close behind him then followed Doc to the other side of the room. When they saw the body lying at Marisha's feet, they both recognized him. It was the frail man that held them up the last time they were here, though he had now acquired two holes in his chest, raw and leaking red. The faint wisp of life that the man previously held onto had left him entirely.

Doc crouched and ran the man's pockets, which was not a huge effort as all he had on was a ragged T-shirt and a tattered pair of dark jeans.

"Jesus, Doc," Marisha said.

Doc came up empty handed. "Sorry," she said, looking away from them.

Marisha went over to the nearest window and peeked through a crack in the boards. "We need to move him."

"Isn't that way too risky right now?" Derby asked.

"Not as risky as letting the stink of him set in. We don't need any more attention drawn here." She stopped on her way back to the body. The sound of skin slapping pavement was approaching the front door. They didn't have time to retreat into the hidden room below so they each found a spot in the corner of the room, behind one of the many stacks of metal and debris.

The door opened loudly. From Derby's position he could peek through a gap in the refuse, and he saw two men enter the room. They looked in a similar state to the dead man: shabby, thin clothing, sunken eyes, and an air of desperation that filled the space around them. The men very quickly found the corpse and began to unceremoniously strip it bare, not speaking a word to each other throughout the process. Once they had secured the clothing off the man's body, they lifted him by the arms and legs and carried him out the door. They let the naked figure drop hard on the pavement outside as they both worked to close the heavy door behind them.

"Well, shit. That takes care of that I guess," Marisha said with a grim look, then led them back down into the Bad Moon hideout leaving the shadow of death in the room above. A presence that was becoming all too familiar in Derby's life. An unwelcome specter that he couldn't seem to shake.

9

A DIRECTION TO CRAWL

IT WAS LATE in the morning when Marisha gathered them all around the shoddy wooden table at the center of the hideout. Derby could see traces of tears in the woman's eyes, a red weariness that crept in around the edges. Still, she carried herself with confidence, showing stability for the group at a time when they desperately needed it.

"We're gonna have to take some risks today," Marisha said apologetically. "I need you all to trust me." The group nodded, encouraging her to continue. She let out a deep sigh. "We're okay down here for now, but we're isolated. We need a way to connect. And we *really* need the keys to our stash at Buck's. That container holds everything we have left in the world."

She paused, turning to Derby and Doc. "There's a good chance they didn't take the HAM from the apartment. The A's would have no use for it."

"The container keys are there as well, under the floorboard in our room," Doc said, looking across at her brother who nodded in agreement.

"Doc and Sticks," Marisha delegated, "I need you two to find a way into the apartment. Get those keys, the HAM if it's still there, and if we're really lucky, they left a portable. Whatever else you can manage that they haven't pilfered."

Doc nodded. "We can sneak in through 312. North facing unit, looks out into the alley. Place has been empty for years. If the A's are still lurking around, I'm betting they won't have eyes on that side."

"It's still *very* dangerous. You'll need to be careful," Marisha said sternly.

"We will," Derby agreed.

"What about the rest of you?" Doc asked.

Marisha rubbed her head. "The other thing we need right now is information. We need to find out what the Gambles are up to, and what—" she paused for a moment clearing a catch in her throat, "what King was onto, who was poking around Gamble House and why. Anything that might help us figure out what the *hell* to do next." She looked across the table at Marv. "You and I are gonna go talk to Jeph."

The older Taylor twin's eyes widened. "Rolling up on Ashes territory after what happened last night? Shit, Maman. Talk about dangerous," Marv said with a faint smirk.

"I know," she said, shaking her head. "Like I said, we've gotta take some risks."

The Soulman nodded his approval. "I'm with ya."

"What about me?" These were the first words that JT had spoken since The Hollow.

Marisha looked at the girl with deep sympathy in her eyes. "You're staying here. These are both very risky jo—"

"I'm going to the apartment with Doc," the girl stated matter-of-factly, making intense eye contact with Marisha.

"JT, I can't—"

"Marisha. I'm going with Doc," she said, staring back at the older woman with a look of pure, unmoving steel.

Marisha opened her mouth as if to push back again, then closed it, reconsidering. She breathed deeply. "Okay," she said, as if reassuring herself. "Okay."

She turned to Doc and Derby. "*Extremely* careful. If it comes down to getting the stuff or getting caught, you get the *hell* out of there." The look on the woman's face was hard. There was nothing even slightly resembling compromise to be found.

They both acknowledged Marisha's instructions. "Got it," Doc said.

There was a moment of silence while they all considered the tasks they had laid out before them. "Food," Marv said. "I'm already starving."

Marisha nodded. "We'll see if Chel can help us out on the way back." She looked around the table at each of them. "We'll figure this out. . .one step at a time."

JT turned and left the table, heading to the far corner of the room where she picked up one of the old, ruddy backpacks that was piled there, and began shaking the dust off it.

The Black Ashes were, by a decent margin, the second most prominent crew in Reed City, behind The Gamble Family. While most crews in town were generational organizations, The Ashes were a newly founded group, like the Bad Moons. Growing up with Obo and Cain Gamble, Jeph had watched his friends take on the responsibility of leading their respective crews, which inspired him to do the same.

While Obo chose not to build the Bad Moon Crew beyond

the small, nucleic family that it was, Jeph made a different choice. Groups almost never set themselves up south of the Kin Line, so when Jeph and his sister Saffi planted the roots of The Black Ashes in the south side, the crew very quickly exploded in size. Within a few years, they had matched the Gambles in members. Though they lagged far behind in power and resources, their numbers counted for enough to earn them a place in the upper echelon of the Reed City pecking order.

The Ashes, being such a large group, and having the southern Reeds largely to themselves, ended up widely spread out with lots of different venues belonging to them dotted around the map, both official and unofficial. Of all those spots, there was one where you could reliably find the Ashes' leadership, Jeph included, either conducting business or unwinding, and that was The Slip. Built into the underside of an overpass in the dead center of the south side, the place didn't proclaim itself at all. There was no advertisement or sign that the unremarkable grey door was anything special. Hidden in the shadow of the large walkway overhead, you had to know about The Slip to find it.

"If things go south in there, get yourself out," Marisha said as they headed down the narrow dirt path that ran beneath the overpass. They both had the hoods of their dark sweaters pulled far down over their faces.

"No way it comes to that, Maman. This is Jeph we're talkin' about," Marv replied.

"No." She stopped a short way from the plain grey door and grabbed The Soulman by the arm. "It's different now, Marv. Don't count on anything being the way it was. It's safest to behave like we're about to enter the lion's den."

Marv nodded and reached under his long black jacket, releasing the safety straps that held his pistols in their sling holsters. They approached the door to The Slip, and Marisha rapped on it with three stabbing knocks. There was a moment of stillness, then the door swung open and a man in a black suit motioned them into the establishment.

The low-ceilinged lounge was dimly lit; every bulb in the place was fitted with a shade of red-tinted glass, diffusing all the light down to a scarlet glow. The light was then filtered one step further through the thick fog of smoke that filled the den.

Straight across from the entrance there was a bar with a man behind it cleaning glasses, but the space between was where the rest of the place's inhabitants were found. Ten or so members of the Ashes were seated around a big circular table in the center, the source of the stifling smog that hung over the room as each of them puffed on either a cigarette or a cigar. At the far end of the table sat the man they were there to see.

Every member of The Black Ashes, the men and the women, wore a black suit with a black shirt and tie, and had black paint on each of their fingernails. Jeph was no exception to this, though his outfit was further accentuated by the black cigarette that sat between his lips, the one JT called 'The Eternal Smoke'; the whole uniform stood out starkly against the man's unnaturally pale skin, and his smoothly shaved head.

When the Bad Moons entered the room, Jeph looked up from the table, and his eyes grew a little wider. "Everyone out," he said in his raspy, ragged voice. The group at the table, all except Saffi, stood without a fuss and made their way to a back room behind the bar. The doorman and the bartender joined in the exodus, leaving only Jeph and his sister in the room with the Bad Moons. While Saffi shared her brother's characteristic pale complexion, where Jeph had no hair, she had plenty. A wild tangle of pitch black framed her pallid face. She eyed Marisha and Marv with a look of pity as they approached the table.

"*What* are you doing here, Marisha?" Jeph asked, his voice thick with disbelief.

Marisha's brow furrowed. "Oh, I'm sorry, are we not *friends,* Jeph?" The Bad Moons stood behind the two chairs across from their compulsory hosts but did not sit.

"*Maman,*" Jeph hissed. "You know you're wanted, right? And not just by the A's but by the Gambles as well."

"That's why we're here." She leaned on the back of the chair in front of her. "We need help."

"*Tch.*" Jeph shook his head, taking a drag from his black

smoke, then resting it on the edge of a red plastic ashtray. "I can't help you."

"Why? Cause you're scared of Ruse Gamble?"

Saffi interjected. "Marisha, come—"

"No, Saf!" She waved the woman off, keeping her attention focused on the leader of the Ashes. "What's he up to, Jeph? And what the *fuck* is that thing in his head?"

"You're damn right I'm scared of him!" The pale man sat forward in his chair, raising his raspy voice. "And you should be too!" They stared at each other for a moment until Jeph looked away, sitting back. "Do you. . ." Jeph sighed, returning his gaze to the Bad Moons. "Do you know where I got this?" He pointed to the cigarette resting on the ashtray nearby.

Marisha and Marv shook their heads.

"I guess I don't really know either," Jeph croaked, leaning forward. "When I got sick, I was sure that was it. Pancreatic. Not much to be done about it. Not down here. So, when I got the letter, I was ready to try anything." Jeph picked up the obsidian cigarette that leaked a small trail of black smoke from its tip. "Ecclesia. That's what they called it. Still got no clue who 'they' even are. The whole thing was mired in secrecy. But they offered me *this.* Said it might help. I was just desperate enough to try it."

He brought the cigarette to his mouth and took a deep

drag. "And it did. Help, that is. Took a few months, but my situation improved. I mean, the thing has destroyed my voice and took all my hair but hell, five years, I'm still here." Jeph took a small silver case out of his pocket, placed the smoke inside and closed it up with the smoke still burning, tucking the gift back inside the folds of his jacket. "That's no small thing."

"Now, I suspect the same benefactor is responsible for Ruse's new trick. I don't understand the how of it, but Ruse. . .he's about to change everything down here. Flip it all upside down, so he says." The man turned his gaze back to Marisha. "You've seen what he can do? Then you know why I believe him. And I *know* you understand that I need to make sure the Ashes end up on the right side of that."

Marisha looked down, clenching her jaw, the muscles flexing on the side of her face. The ink that formed the sun shape on the back of her right hand stretched under the tension of her squeeze. "They murdered him right in front of us." She looked back across the table at the pale siblings. "My husband and your *friend*. Arthur Rook cut his throat and let him *bleed* and *choke* on the floor of The Hollow." The Ashes shifted in their seats and looked anywhere else in the room except at her. "We couldn't do anything but watch."

She let the moment sink in, pushing off the chair back to her full height. "Before they butchered him, Ruse was talking about someone sniffing around Gamble House, implying that King had something to do with it. Said he came to you about it, that the guy was former Ashes." Jeph met her eyes again. "Who was it Jeph?" The man ran his hand over his stark white head and breathed deeply.

Marisha grit her teeth. "The bastard took *everything* from us. Didn't even have the courtesy to finish the job, just cut us off at the legs and left us to crawl. Now, you can't help us, that's fine, but at least give me a name so we can have a goddamn direction to crawl in." The last sentence carried with it the closest thing to desperation that Marisha dared to show the siblings.

Jeph was silent until Saffi nudged her brother gently. "Donovan Notch." The name croaked out of his ragged throat as though it was never meant to escape.

"Notch?" Marisha asked, sharing a brief look of surprise with Marv. "Well. . .that's something at least." She nodded to The Soulman and they turned, heading for the door.

"Marisha," Jeph called out just as the woman opened the front door, letting the midday light flood into The Slip. "Far as I'm concerned, this conversation didn't happen. But this is it. Do *not* come back here again. Going forward, I see you out there? The Gambles will know."

Marisha smiled looking out the door, then turned her head back toward the siblings. "Thanks, Jeph." The Bad Moons let the grey door slam shut behind them and stood for a minute on the unassuming doorstep in the shadow of the overpass.

"Shit," Marv said.

"He gave us Notch. It's something," Marisha said. "We can start there, see where it leads us."

"Nah, it ain't that," he replied, shaking his head. "I just lost a bet is all."

Marisha led the way as they ventured back out into the hostile streets of The Reeds, where danger was closing in, and their list of friends dwindled by the hour.

10
WHATEVER THAT'S WORTH

DOC BROUGHT THE butt of her pistol down hard onto the window latch, cracking the white plastic. The fire escape they were crouched on rattled a little from the impact. A second, solid blow was enough to break the latch off completely, releasing the lock. She slid the window up, holding it open for Derby to climb through.

There had been no sign of A's presence around the front of the building when they surveyed the area. In the name of caution, however, they followed the plan that Doc had outlined back in the hideout and approached the apartment from the less-exposed north side alley. As the younger Taylor twin had predicted, so far, they'd had an uncomplicated path into the building.

Derby stepped through the window into unit 312 and realized Doc had also been right about the apartment's vacancy. The place was entirely empty and looked as though it had been that way for a long time. The floors were bare, and a thick layer of dust covered all the baseboards and surfaces. The room smelled stale and neglected.

JT crawled over the dusty sill next, with Doc bringing up the rear, letting the window fall closed softly behind them.

The youngest Bad Moon stifled a cough. "Nasty," she whispered, leading the group across the empty room to the entrance of the unit. JT reached for the deadbolt on the front door but was intercepted by Doc who gently grabbed the girl's arm, giving her a look of caution. Doc stepped in front of the group and unlocked the deadbolt herself, cracking the door open slowly, just enough that she could peek out into the hallway. After a moment she turned back and nodded, leading them out of 312 and down the empty corridor.

When they reached the door to their apartment, they found it ajar. There was a hole in the frame where the lock had once engaged, and two thick yellow ribbons were strewn across the entrance in the shape of an 'X'. The Bad Moons ducked under the tape and entered unit 315.

The place had been turned over pretty thoroughly. Most

drawers in the kitchen had been left open with their contents scrambled, all of the furniture was out of place, the pool table had been knocked over and the colored balls were scattered across the floor. The A's had done a decent number on their home, though it didn't look like they'd actually removed much of anything from the residence. The HAM radio that they were hoping to retrieve was still there, on the floor in the corner, the table it once sat on lying knocked over a few feet away.

"Let's be quick. Sticks, grab the radio," Doc said as she scurried across the apartment and down the hallway toward the bedrooms. While Derby stepped through the wreckage of the living room, JT made a beeline for the kitchen and began rummaging through one of the drawers. Derby reached the HAM and bent down to inspect it. The radio didn't seem damaged, but turning the dial on the front did not bring the device to life as he would've expected. Turning it over he found the battery compartment in the back of the device was empty. He looked up and watched JT pull something from the drawer she was searching through and stuff it into her pocket. The girl turned, looking around the house, and walked slowly over to the living room.

"No batteries," Derby said. She shot him a dismissive glance and knelt down by the overturned pool table, picking up the eight ball and rolling it around in her hand. The girl hadn't said much since The Hollow, but she seemed to be making a point of not acknowledging Derby's existence. He understood why.

The radio looked like it might not be small enough to fit inside the backpack that Derby had brought, but he managed to squeeze it in, just barely able to close the zipper around it. Doc emerged from her bedroom dangling a ring of keys in front of her. "Got em. Looks like they took all our portables though. How's the HAM?" she asked.

"It's missing batteries, seems fine otherwise," Derby replied, throwing the backpack over his shoulders. Doc made her way into the kitchen and hopped up onto the counter, opening one of the high cupboards. She reached around for a second, then pulled out an old container that was overflowing with batteries and proceeded to dump the contents into her backpack.

"Might all be dead, but worth a shot," she said, hopping back down. Derby looked around the room and couldn't help but feel sad. He hadn't lived there for very long, but he felt the violation, nonetheless. He couldn't imagine what the others must feel. Though the ransacking of their home wasn't the tallest tragedy of the last twenty-four hours, it still stung. In one night, Ruse Gamble had managed to eviscerate almost every measure of safety the Bad Moons had built.

"Alright, let's go. We shouldn't linger," Doc said, walking carefully up to the entrance. Derby snapped out of his thoughts and joined Doc at the front door where she had her head stuck out into the hallway, scanning for danger. JT stood, pocketing the eight ball she had been fiddling with and joined them as well. The corridor was still clear, so they followed Doc quietly back to unit 312.

Derby entered the deserted apartment last, and as he closed the door behind them, he heard the faint *DING* of the elevator from the other end of the floor. Doc hopped out the window first, rattling the fire escape as she started making her way down the ladder. JT stepped out next, holding the window open for Derby to follow.

"Don't move!" Derby spun around and saw a man he didn't recognize in the doorway with a gun out, aimed right at him. In the swell of things, Derby had forgotten to lock the door behind them. The man, who was slowly stepping further into the apartment seemed nervous, a glistening layer of sweat covered his forehead.

Derby didn't think too much about what he did next, it just happened. He dropped the backpack with the radio inside off his shoulders, letting it fall through the window and onto the fire escape next to JT. "Go!" he said over his shoulder, reaching behind him and slamming the window shut.

The unfamiliar man fumbled at his belt trying to grab his radio which fell to the floor. Amazed he hadn't been shot yet, and taking advantage of this stumble, Derby rushed toward the man and tackled him to the ground. As they hit the dusty floor in a crumple, the gun flew from the man's hand sliding across the room. Derby was the shorter of the two and his opponent, even though the man wasn't much bulkier than him, had a clear strength advantage. They wrestled for a few moments before the man got on top of Derby and rained a punch down onto his face. He felt the heat of the impact under his eye immediately. The man pulled back to punch him again, but before he could release the blow, an arm slipped around his neck from behind and pulled him backwards.

Derby sat up and saw JT wrapped around the man like a backpack, squeezing his neck tight. The man's face grew redder by the second. In an effort to clear the girl from his neck, he jerked his head backwards, so that the back of his skull made contact with her face. A sickening crack sounded through the room and JT slumped to the floor, blood flowing freely from her nose. The man dropped to one knee, gasping for air and looked across the room for his weapon. Derby's gaze found the pistol at the same time.

They both scrambled for the gun, reaching it simultaneously, each trying to wrestle it from the other's grasp. The man drove a hand sharply into Derby's throat which caused him to reflexively bring his hands there as he started coughing. The man grabbed the now uncontested gun and aimed it down at Derby, taking a deep breath.

CRACK. The man fell sideways to the floor like a sack of bricks, completely limp. JT stood there with the black eight ball in her hand; her face covered in blood from her broken nose. Derby sat up, still coughing intermittently from the jab to the throat.

"Thanks," he croaked. The bloodied girl nodded, wiping her nose on her sleeve and helping him to his feet. Just then, the window slid open, and Doc crawled through.

She took in the scene around her. "What the fuck happened?" She ran over to JT who was still working with her sleeve to stem the blood flow. Doc tried to get a better look at the girl's face but was quickly swatted away.

"I'm fine," JT said. Doc knew better than to press it and stepped over to the man who lay very still, a small puddle of blood was now pooling under his head.

"He's a Gamble," Doc said. "He was at the cemetery the night we met Ruse."

"Is he dead?" JT asked.

"Probably," Doc replied. "We need to leave now. There's no way he was in the area alone."

They left through the window, Derby picking up the backpack with the HAM on the way out. They didn't encounter any Gambles or A's on their way back to the south side, but to be safe they took a detour to the west end and then cut back across the Kin Line, hoping to shake any unwanted followers.

After seeing their old home in such disarray, the last thing they wanted to do was jeopardize the final sliver of safety they knew.

Derby didn't notice how hungry he had been until the meal was done. Marisha and Marv had braved The Drum on their way back to the hovel, visiting Aunt Chel, who filled their bags with whatever food and drink she was able to spare. After exchanging updates on their respective tasks over dinner, the Bad Moons found themselves full and tired as they sat on the mattresses at the back of the hideout, the savory smell of the meal still lingering in the air.

"So, I guess add The Black Ashes to the shit-list," Doc said, grabbing another pair of batteries. She was going through the pile of potential she had grabbed from the apartment, trying to bring the HAM to life.

"Just put the whole Reeds on there at this point," JT said, sitting against the wall at the top of her bedding. The young girl's broken nose had begun to blacken her eyes and there was a congested tone to her voice.

"Not the whole place. Chel came through for us big today," Marisha corrected. "And it's not like Jeph gave us *nothing.*"

"Ay, we got enough to last a while now thanks to Chel, but we need a plan, Maman," Marv said, getting up from his mattress and walking over to where JT sat. "Before I forget." He reached into the pouch that hung off the sling that held his pistols, and pulled out two coins, tossing them into JT's lap.

It took a second for the girl to crawl through her own mind and find the reason she was getting paid. "No fucking way," she said, with an incredulous smile.

"*Lucky* guess," Marv said, tossing himself back down on the bedding next to where his sister was discarding another pair of batteries that had failed to revive the radio.

The young girl's laugh caused her nose to scrunch up which made her wince. "I knew it, man," she whispered through her discomfort.

Marisha smiled at JT. "That plan, Marv. I'm working on it," she said, closing her eyes. "I'm gonna pay a visit to Donovan Notch tomorrow, see what he can tell us. See if he found anything while snooping around Gamble House."

"And what if he did? What do we do with that information?" Doc asked. "It's not like we can take on the Gambles ourselves."

"Says who?" JT piped up.

Doc smirked. "JT, we barely got away from *one* Gamble today."

"Yeah, no thanks to you! Took your sweet time gett—"

"Okay, enough. Please," Marisha said calmly, rubbing her

temples. “Doc’s right we can’t take the fight to the Gambles directly. But maybe Notch knows something that can give us another way.” She looked down at the youngest Bad Moon. “You’ll just have to trust me.” JT shrugged Marisha off, looking straight ahead in silence.

BZZT. The HAM flared to life; Doc had found a pair of batteries with some life left. “Ha!” she exclaimed, turning the dial on the front of the device until the frequency read ‘7.15’. The signal of the radio became clear and smooth sounds filled the room, bringing along with them a sense of calm.

“Ayy.” The Soulman smiled. “In A Sentimental Mood, Duke Ellington and John Coltrane, 1963.” He closed his eyes and sat back, the rest of the group following suit, just listening for a while. Derby closed his eyes. It was the first moment that had felt remotely peaceful since their world had been pulled out from under them.

Derby awoke slowly with a heavy crick in his neck, having passed out with his head propped against the wall. The room was quiet save for the light snoring of the sleeping Bad Moons around him and the faint sounds of soft music coming from the HAM that sat by the Taylor twins. They must have all fallen asleep listening to the music.

He shifted himself down into his bed proper, rubbing his eyes, and noticed that the mattress next to him was empty. A quick, bleary-eyed scan of the area revealed a small shape, sitting cross-legged at the bottom of the ladder across the room. He sat up and contemplated for a moment whether he should disturb the girl, ultimately deciding he might not get a better opportunity to apologize.

He made his way quietly across the room so as not to disturb the others, and sat down next to JT, resting his arms on his bent knees in front of him. The girl stared at the hatch above them, not acknowledging his presence. After a few minutes of quiet he broke the silence. "I'm sorry. . .really sorry. . .whatever that's worth."

The girl maintained her gaze above. "It's okay," she said after a moment or two. He nodded, then noticed that JT was holding something: a small intricately carved wooden crest attached to a loop of twine. Her thumbs were slowly tracing and re-tracing the pattern that was carved into the trinket.

"Is that what you took from the apartment?" he asked softly.

The girl nodded. "I don't remember much of my birth parents. King and Marisha took me in when I was five." She paused. "They didn't die or anything. Well, maybe they're dead now, I dunno. I guess they just decided they didn't want the burden anymore?" The girl shrugged. "So, they took me to The

Drum one day and just. . .left me there. Gotta respect the balls on 'em." She smirked.

"Anyway, I was lucky enough to end up here, but I could *not* stand being alone. Trauma or whatever. So, King made me this, a few months in." She looked down at the necklace in her hands. "Carved it himself. Said that as long as I wore it, I'd be safe. You know, shit you say to kids." She smiled. "But it helped. I felt safe." Tears had welled in the girl's eyes but hadn't fallen yet.

"Why was it in the drawer?" Derby asked curiously.

JT wiped her eyes before the tears could escape and shrugged. "Got too cool for it a couple years back. But now it's the only piece of him I have left. Cause no matter how long I sit here, he's not coming down that ladder."

She looped the twine over her head and let the carving fall around her neck. "You made a *really* dumb mistake, Sticks, but King forgave you. So, I do too."

They sat in the stillness of the dark hovel, the soft sound of the blues doing its best to fill the space around them. "He liked you a lot ya know," the girl said, looking at Derby.

"Me?" he questioned.

The girl rolled her eyes. "Come on, Sticks. This isn't The Ashes where all you need is a pulse to get in. King kept things really tight. The fact that you're here means he thought you were special."

Derby shook his head, looking up at the hatch above them. "I don't know if anything special can survive up there. This place just hunts it down and. . .snuffs it out."

"Grim," she said with a half-smile. "I dunno." She looked down at the carving around her neck. "I think *this* is pretty special. And God help the person *or* the place that tries to take it from me."

Derby smiled.

BZZT. "Hello?"

They jumped, startled by the sudden sound of a woman's voice coming from the radio. The rest of the Bad Moons jumped awake; Marv, being closest to the radio, groggily reached over, turning the volume on the HAM up and grabbing the transmitter. "Nat?"

"Marv! Jesus, I've been trying to get through since. . .I had no idea. You have to believe that I didn't know."

"We don't have to believe anything Natalia," Marisha said, the whole crew was now huddled around the HAM. "After what your brother has done?"

"I know. He's gone off the deep end. And it's only going to get worse. Listen, I can't say anything more here, and I don't expect you

to trust me, but. . .I'm going to stop Ruse, and I need your help. I think you could use mine too."

Marisha replied exasperatedly. "Natalia, we're not just going to—"

There was a loud noise on the other end of the transmission. *"Tomorrow night, nine o'clock, Aunt Chel's place. Please show up."*

The channel went quiet. Everyone was wide awake now.

"Okay, there's no way that isn't a trap, right?" JT asked. "Ruse is obviously using her to get to us."

"What if it's not though?" Doc said. "We don't have many options here. This could be our way forward."

"I don't think she was lying," Marv chimed in. "Nat's a lot of things, but whatever Ruse has become? She ain't that."

Derby spoke up. "JT's not wrong. It could be a trap. Feels like we just went through this."

The group sat silent for a moment. "What you thinkin', Maman?" Marv asked.

Marisha breathed deep. "I want to believe that Nat's trying to help. But it's a *big* risk. If she's trying to set us up, or even if she isn't but Ruse is onto her, she'll lead him right to us. And he won't make the mistake of playing with his food again." She considered the group. "On the other hand, Doc's right. We don't have many options. But we'd be foolish to run in there blind." Marisha thought for a moment.

"She said to meet her at Chel's place. Middle of The Drum, lots of people, lots of places to blend in. I'll go in and meet with Natalia. *Alone*."

Doc interjected. "Maman, there's no way—"

"The rest of you will *stay here*. Not up for discussion." She looked around sternly. "If things go bad, I'll vanish, try to make it back here if I can."

Derby wanted to protest, but he could see where Marisha was coming from. They truly didn't have a lot of options.

Marisha continued. "I said we were gonna have to take some risks. This is a heavy risk, no doubt. But if there's a shot that Natalia can help us find a way to stop the bastard. . .that's a risk we have to take." She looked around at them, setting her jaw.

"Ruse Gamble set our world on fire last night, let's return the favor."

11
ALL THAT I ASK

THREE MONTHS AGO

"RENAISSANCE?"

Natalia had always been smart. Maybe the smartest of the Gamble siblings. Always perceptive and always asking the right questions. Cain had seen it from the time his sister was a child, and he could see it now as she sat across the desk from him, holding the little black card.

His office was modest. The heavy oak desk where the two of them sat was the centerpiece, surrounded by a sea of carpeted floor that ran in every direction up to the large bookshelves that lined the walls on all sides.

"Ah, that's nothing. A dead opportunity." He reached across and took the card from his sister. It was almost entirely black except for the one word that Natalia had just spoken, written in white, block letters on both sides.

"Sorry," Natalia said, fiddling with the rings on her fingers.

"Don't be," he replied, tucking the card away in one of his desk drawers. "I killed it."

"Oh?" Her eyebrows rose slightly, followed by a look of realization. "Oh. *That's* what you and Ruse have been at each other's throats over for the past few weeks."

Cain laughed. "Feels like that's been us more often than not lately. This Renaissance thing was just. . ." His vibrant blue eyes looked distant as he ruffled his beard, sighing deeply. "Anyway, you had something for me?"

Natalia nodded. "I think we should re-open Gamble House," she said nonchalantly.

Cain smiled. "Nat," he said with a tone that implied her statement was unrealistic, "we don't have the resources."

"Not to what it was before," she said. "At least not right away. I'm saying we open a few beds. Turn the lights and the heat on. Start there."

The elder Gamble eyed her with a puzzled look. "We'd need to staff it."

"Minimally. Like I said, start small, build it out."

He shook his head. "I don't know, Nat. It's a tough sell. I pushed so hard already this year for the Market Exchange, *genius* idea of mine, and that went belly up."

"That *was* a good idea," Natalia said. "Unfortunately, there's always a catch when it comes to business with The Uppers."

Cain rubbed his temple. "I need to give the boys something solid to sink their teeth into now. Something sure."

Natalia paused for a moment, he could see the girl considering her next words carefully. "This place is fading, Cain," she said calmly. "The Reeds has never exactly been a font of fortune but it's. . .it's worse than ever. I know you can see that. If things are getting tight for *us*, imagine how it is for the other crews. And the south siders?" She shook her head. "It can't continue like this. Things won't hold. And Gamble House is a looming reminder of that. Hanging over the city, symbolizing our…decomposition." She shrugged. "We can change the message."

Cain sighed. His sister was smart. And she was onto something. "I'll consider it."

"Thank you. That's all that I ask," she said with a smile.

"Between you and me, it's heaps better than the last proposal I had to sit through," Cain said, shaking his head. Natalia raised an eyebrow inquisitively.

"Your brother wants to kidnap and ransom the Fifth Council at the next Tithe."

Natalia's eyes narrowed. "That seems like a great way to get us all killed," she said, concerned.

"I agree." Cain leaned back in his chair, rubbing his eyes. "The day I can't do this anymore Nat, *you're* taking the reins."

She laughed. "Good luck breaking that to Ruse. Talk about a tough sell."

Cain smiled and stood up. "Alright, let's go meet the new Bad Moon kid."

The young man was faded. Cain could see it in the way he carried himself. A slightly hunched posture, avoidant eyes, as if the world had forced him to submit. This was what Natalia had been talking about. The fading of The Reeds and its people.

"Cain, I'd like you to meet Derby 'Sticks' O'Malley, newest member of The Bad Moon Crew." King spoke from across their usual table in The Hollow, gesturing to the wisp of a man standing behind him, who nodded nervously.

"A pleasure to meet you, Mr. O'Malley," Cain said, eyeing the man curiously. He let the room hang in silence for a moment then continued. “Tell me, Derby, what is one thing that you need? Something you don’t already have.”

The young man stammered a bit, looking around the room nervously.

“It can be anything, big or small,” Cain continued, “It’s a question I like to ask the people I’m letting into the family. Helps me understand them better. And the Bad Moons are an extension of The Gamble Family.”

He felt Ruse shift uncomfortably to his right. His brother hated it when he included the Bad Moons in this way. “The Taylor twins, for example, answered ‘Time’ and ‘Coin’. One answer each,” he said, gesturing to the twins sitting on the table behind King. “Quite the pragmatic pair. I’ll let you figure out who answered which. Then there was young JT.” Cain eyed the youngest Bad Moon with a smile. “I believe your exact words were ‘For you to stop asking me questions.’” Cain chuckled. “Girl was what, five?” he asked, gesturing to King who nodded in response. “So, Mr. O’Malley, what do *you* need?”

After a moment of stillness, Derby answered. “I—I don’t know, sir. I don’t have a good answer.” He said, retreating into his defeated posture. “Sorry.”

Cain smiled. “Don’t apologize, son. Tell you what, you think about it, and give me an answer the next time I see you.” Derby nodded.

"Speaking of thinking on things, Tithe is coming up in a few months," King said, looking at Cain expectantly.

"So I've been reminded," Cain replied, glancing at Ruse.

"Have you considered talking to The Fifth?" King asked.

Cain leaned back in his chair. "The Fifth has never negotiated on Tithe. Not that I know of."

"Has anyone ever tried? We don't have the resources to keep up Cain. Something has to give. And if we don't push back, that something will be *us*," the Bad Moon leader asserted.

Ruse piped up. "They won't negotiate with us. They'd need to view us as human to entertain that idea."

King shifted his gaze to Ruse. "What, then? We just roll over and bleed ourselves dry?"

"Not at all. I think we need a more. . .deliberate approach," Ruse said with a tilt of his head.

"*Ruse*," Cain said with a cautioning tone.

The younger Gamble continued anyway. "I wonder how The Uppers would respond if the Fifth never returned from their visit? I imagine they might waive Tithe altogether in exchange for the safe return of their beloved council."

Cain closed his eyes, sighing, and across the table from him, King eyed Ruse with an incredulous stare.

"You're right, Ruse, they might waive Tithe," King said. "And then, once the Fifth was safe back up top, they would return to make an example of us. And that example would be *severe*, to discourage anything of the sort from happening again."

Ruse scoffed. "We're not powerless."

"Aren't we?" King raised his voice. "These people are *broken*. If we have power, it is nowhere near the surface. When was the last time you visited the south side brother? You want them to *resist*?" He paused, running his hands through his hair. "Inviting conflict now will *not* stoke their power, it will snuff out whatever spark is left. We need to help them find the fire."

Ruse opened his mouth to speak again but Cain interjected. "That's enough for today. We'll discuss this further next week." Ruse gritted his teeth, and King looked ready to protest, but they both remained silent.

Cain smiled and turned his gaze back to the new kid. "Mr. O'Malley, don't forget to think on an answer to my question. I look forward to it."

"King's right, you know, to have the concerns that he does," Ruse said, shaking out the match he had just used to light his cigar. "It's a pretty grim proposal from where they're sitting," he said, exhaling a large plume of white smoke that dispersed and filled the air of the office.

Cain could see the ambition in his brother's eyes, across the desk from him. It burned so bright, he could barely see any color there. Ruse leaned forward. "But Cain, with the help of Renaissance, we could—"

"Ruse, please," the elder Gamble said wearily. "It's done. We've exhausted this conversation. My decision is final."

Ruse exhaled another cloud of smoke. "So, we reject freedom."

Cain sighed. "Quite the opposite brother, we reject servitude. An offer like this does not come without a price, whether or not it's advertised. You think these people just handout power like this freely?"

Ruse gritted his teeth. "Maybe they can see our potential."

"They see us as guinea pigs Ruse. Test subjects. So that they don't have to take the risk. You said it yourself, they don't see us as human." Cain rubbed his temples. "We don't prove them wrong by taking their poison."

Ruse nodded slowly, glancing at Arthur Rook who stood at the room's edge, leaning against one of the bookshelves that lined the wall. "And is that my brother speaking or the Bad Moon King?"

Cain looked up and gave Ruse a serious stare. "*Careful,* brother." He looked around the room and leaned back in his chair. "Even putting aside the unspoken cost, you've heard the proposition. You know what we'd have to do. Could you *really* do that Ruse? To any person? Despite assurances, we have no idea what sort of fate we'd be signing them up for. How could you ask that of anyone?"

"I would gladly volunteer, Mr. Gamble," Arthur said from the edge of the room.

"I would *never* allow that, Arthur," the Gamble leader said, eyeing his bodyguard with a look of caution. "As I said, it's done. I've already let them know we're not interested." He looked across the desk at his brother, and his colorless eyes. "I appreciate your ambition, Ruse. It can get you far and will do it fast." Cain leaned over the desk. "But temper it. I beg you. If you let it, it will burn you out and leave you blind."

12
HIT WHAT'S IN FRONT OF YOU

DONOVAN NOTCH had been dead for a while, and the air in the small apartment was starting to take on the stench of his corpse. The place felt like a shipwreck. As if the streets of the south side, where they had come from, were the ocean floor, and instead of the door to Notch's upended home, they had stepped through a hole in the hull of an ancient vessel, into a dark, damp tomb. Everything in the home sat at an odd angle,, floating in a spot it didn't seem to belong.

Strewn among the wreckage, tangled up in the shattered remnants of a table, was the sprawled figure of Donovan Notch; eyes open, staring eerily at the ceiling. His throat had been cut, a similar wound to the one that King had received at

The Hollow. Blood covered the man's clothes and had pooled around him, now mostly dried. Derby choked on the smell as they approached the body.

"Gambles got to him," Marisha said, kneeling next to the man.

"Did you know him well?" Derby asked through his sweater which he had pulled up to cover his face from the nose down.

"Not particularly," she answered. "He was close to Jeph, and he always got along with King." She furrowed her brow and picked up a bloodstained polaroid from the man's chest. A handful of photos had been scattered over Notch's body. She examined the picture briefly, then handed it to Derby.

The image was dark and a bit blurry, but Derby was able to make out Ruse Gamble standing at the entrance of Gamble House, waving a large truck through the tall iron gates. A quick scan of the other photos showed that they were all taken from a similar angle and captured the unmarked truck pulling up to the doors of the old gothic building. Other scenes displayed large crates being unloaded from the back of the truck and into the defunct hospital.

A single odd item stood out among the bloody polaroids that decorated the man's body. A black card, with one word printed on it in white, block letters: **RENAISSANCE**. Marisha picked the card up and turned it over, finding an identical backside.

Derby placed the photo back into the loose pile, coughing as the stench of death found the back of his throat again. "What does that mean?" he asked gesturing to the strange card.

Marisha shook her head. "No idea." She gathered up all the photos and flipped through the stack, studying them. "No markings on the truck or the crates, no recognizable faces other than Ruse. . .something's going on at Gamble House."

Derby looked confused. "This is evidence. . .or at least it's something," he said. "Why would they just leave it like this for anyone to find?"

Marisha shrugged. "A challenge, maybe?" she suggested, tucking the stack of photos into her jacket pocket along with the small black card. She ran her fingers gently over Notch's cold eyelids, rolling them shut, covering up his empty stare. "Even without that thing in his neck, Ruse has always thought himself above everyone else. Untouchable." She turned from the dead man to Derby. "It's a taunt. What are *we* gonna do with this that could possibly shake *him*?" she asked, patting her jacket pocket. "I honestly don't know."

"We have to do something," Derby said. Marisha raised her eyebrows slightly, surprised at his assertiveness.

"No matter how much you guys say this was all inevitable, I still feel responsible." Derby let his head hang. "Like I'm the reason King's gone, and I've polluted your world with my cloud of. . .bad luck, I guess." He looked back up at Marisha. "The kind of luck that gets people killed."

"It's not your fault, Sticks, and it's definitely not luck," she said, shaking her head. "Calling it luck absolves Ruse Gamble of responsibility. These are the consequences of his actions. And he—"

"It's okay, Maman. You don't have to reassure me." He paused and met the woman's eyes. "But let me come with you to meet Natalia tonight."

"Sticks, if it's a trap—"

"Then you won't be alone. Please, it's the least I can do. After everything."

Marisha sighed. "Alright." She reached out and patted him on the shoulder, then stood up. "Come on, the others should be getting back from Buck's soon." Derby stood and followed the woman to the door. It felt wrong, leaving the man there to decay and to fade, or to be scavenged by the south siders who would happily use him up, but they couldn't risk any higher level of courtesy. So, they left Notch and his tiny apartment the way they found them: Sinking.

POP. POP.

The rubber bullets whipped through the air in the Bad Moon hideout and smacked against the concrete wall next to the yellow and wood cabinet. A makeshift wooden target had been fixed overtop of the glass inlay, hooded by the old wood. A target that each of Derby's shots had missed entirely.

"You gotta breathe, dude," Doc said. "Holding your breath like that makes you all tense. And remember your base." She adjusted Derby's feet with her own. "Strong base, steady breath. Try again."

He brought the training pistol up once more and did his best to follow Doc's instructions. *POP. POP. POP.* This time, the bullets struck around the outer edges of the target.

"Ay, much better, Sticks," she said, patting him on the back. "If you're gonna put yourself in danger tonight, you at least need to be able to hit what's in front of you." She winked. Derby handed the pistol to Doc, then walked across the room to collect the rubber bullets that were scattered on the ground around the target.

POP. POP. POP. POP. POP. Five more pellets flew through the air in quick succession, and all five smacked home in the dead center of the bullseye. Doc smiled and tucked the training pistol into her belt. After picking up the last of the dummy bullets, Derby spotted Marv tinkering with something in the corner.

"What's that?" Derby asked as he approached The Soulman.

Marv looked up. "Portable," he said, showing Derby the handheld radio. "Grabbed it up from the container, since our good ones got swiped. Forgot we had this clunker in storage, stopped working a few years back." He continued to poke at the device. "Could really come in handy now."

"You know how to fix it?" Derby asked.

Marv shrugged. "I'm figuring it out. Think I'm close." He unplugged a small wire inside the device and plugged it into a different spot, turning the dial on the front to no avail.

Derby looked confused. "How?"

Marv raised an eyebrow as he re-positioned another wire. "Hm?"

"How do you just. . .figure it out?"

The Soulman smiled. "No secret. It's just movement, Sticks. Like anything, you're not always gonna know where to go, but you ain't never gonna get anywhere standing still." He tried the dial again with no result. "You might have to take a few wrong turns, maybe break a few things along the way." He unplugged a different wire this time and routed it into a different spot. "But if you just start *moving.*" He turned the dial expectantly and the radio gave him nothing, the tall man shrugged. "You'll get there eventually."

"Alright, huddle up," Marisha called out. Derby and Marv joined the group as they all trickled over to the center of the hovel, gathering around the wooden table there, and waited for the woman to speak.

"Let's go over this one more time," Marisha said. "Sticks and I are heading to Chel's place at nine to meet Natalia. We'll get there early and do a sweep of the area. The HAM is set to 7.15, the rest of you will *stay here* and wait for us to contact you. Any luck with the portable?" she asked, looking at Marv who was still prodding the device.

"Workin' on it," he said.

Marisha nodded. "Worst case we'll have Chel's HAM if we need it. *Under no circumstances will you come after us.* Understood?" She looked around the table for confirmation. Slowly, one by one, they all nodded in agreement. "Okay. If things go south, we'll do our best to get out of there and make it back. If we *do* need you, if Natalia really does want to help, we'll signal on the radio. We can't count on it being secure, so we'll need a key."

"King," JT said, without hesitation.

Marisha nodded. "King it is. You hear that name, you come meet us. Thankfully, you all were able to grab more than just Doc's peashooters from the container," she gestured over to a small stack of weapons, ammunition, and foodstuffs piled in the far corner, "so you can come prepared." She paused. "Any questions?"

No one said anything for a moment while Doc walked over to the small pile of weapons they had picked up from Buck's, bringing a pair of pistols back to the group and handing one each to Derby and Marisha. "You two will need to be prepared too. In case shit goes wrong in The Drum."

Derby held the pistol, noticing immediately how much heavier it felt in his hand than the comparatively flimsy training guns. He tucked the weighty steel into his belt.

BZZT. The radio in Marv's hands buzzed to life suddenly, much to the group's delight. "Ay, *movement*, Sticks," The Soulman said, winking at Derby.

Derby smiled and checked his watch; the hands were approaching seven. He hesitated for a moment, then made a decision. "I'll meet you in The Drum at eight thirty, Maman," he said, leaving the circle and heading for the hatch that led out of the hovel. "There's something I have to do first."

The group was staring at him with collective confusion. "Are you serious?" JT asked.

He paused at the bottom of the ladder. "I'm not gonna do anything stupid. Not again. I promise. I'll be careful." They continued to stare. "Look, I know this is a big ask, given the circumstances, but I need you all to trust me. Please." He looked around the room imploringly.

Marisha nodded warily. "Do what you need to do, Sticks. The Drum. Eight thirty. *Don't* be late."

Doc walked over to him and lifted his sweater, grabbing the pistol and checking the safety. "Safety off first, if you need to use it," she said pointing to the small button at the back of the weapon and then tucking it back into his belt. "Careful, Sticks," she said, eyeing him worriedly. He nodded and climbed the ladder, exiting the hideout through the hatch above.

Derby could see the whole east side of Paisley Street from the corner where he stood, shielded from the rain by the awning of a closed-up market. He tugged his hood further over his face and checked his watch which read quarter after seven. During his walk up from the south side, he had considered, many times, turning around or heading straight to The Drum to wait for Marisha. But instead, he found himself here, on this corner, where he had intended to be.

The street was sparsely populated, most shops had either closed or were closing soon. The few that were still open had steady streams of traffic heading in and out. Derby was focused on a small market across the street from where he was posted up. A short, narrow building that was squeezed between two taller structures, with a sign on the front door reading **OPEN**. He observed the front of the shop for a while, watching people enter, spend some time inside, and then leave with a paper bag or two in hand. The little shop that held his attention sold a variety of things from food to clothes to personal hygiene products. People came here for what they needed to survive. And the man who owned the place provided it to them for as cheap as he possibly could.

Wave after wave of customers entered and then exited the building. People who seemed to be happy. He was beginning to forget what that felt like. Something about watching the world move on the dusty street was hypnotic. Derby checked his watch again, it was almost eight o'clock, time had completely escaped him. He'd been standing on the corner for almost an hour and would need to leave for The Drum soon. His heart began to race, and a thin film of sweat formed over his hands and on his forehead. If he was gonna do this, it would have to be now. His vision began to grey around the edges and just as he was about to cross the street, the owner of the shop came outside. The older man was unassuming, short and round, with white hair and a pair of thin-framed glasses. He wore a white apron and had a shabby-looking broom in his hands with which he began sweeping the mat in front of the door along with the surrounding area.

Derby was frozen. Every thought in his mind was urging him forward, to cross the street and talk to the man, but his body would not cooperate. He stood there, panic-stricken, breathing erratically while the man carried out his end of the day chores in a pleasant manner, striking up a friendly conversation with the owner of the neighboring shop who was closing up his own front.

Derby could not fathom how this man could be smiling, how he could be going about his day like this. Continuing on.

It was so unbelievable to him that it didn't seem real. Finally, the man retreated into his tiny shop, and once inside, flipped the sign on the front door so that it read **CLOSED**.

That was it. He had missed his chance. This realization caused his anxiety to subside; his heart returned to a normal rhythm, and his vision opened back up. Derby thought about how unsure he was of what the next few hours would hold and how he may not get another chance to come back. That thought reminded him to check his watch which now read ten after eight. He needed to go.

Turning briskly, he left the corner of Paisley Street behind and headed for The Drum, feeling an overwhelming sense of relief that nothing had come of this errand as he headed toward a very risky and potentially dangerous meeting with Natalia Gamble.

13
EVEN THE TREES KNOW BETTER

"SHE WAS HERE this morning?"

"Ay, popped in just before I opened," Aunt Chel said, "all covered up and secretive, asked if you all could meet here tonight. Said it was urgent. I said o' course, but I'd like to know what's goin' on." The older woman looked expectantly at Marisha who stood leaning on the counter of the cramped store.

"I take it Natalia didn't elaborate," Marisha said.

Chel shook her head. "Just apologized for the secrecy and hurried off."

Marisha sighed and proceeded to give Aunt Chel an abridged rundown of everything that had gone on over the past few days. Derby listened in while he set the handheld radio that Marisha had brought along to channel 7.15 and clipped it onto his belt.

They had done a sweep of The Drum before entering Chel's place but found no sign of the Gamble Crew or any other cause for alarm in the area. Still, Derby eyed the front door of the shop warily, half expecting Ruse and his lackeys to come barreling through. There were shelves stacked along every possible wall of the store, including the front, so you couldn't see into or out of the place except for a very small window on the door itself.

"That bastard!"

Marisha had finished catching Chel up and the woman was visibly disturbed. "O' course I knew that what I been seein' on the news was a sham, but this? Oh, sweet Obo." Tears welled up at the edges of the woman's milky eyes. "I'm so sorry, Maman."

Derby kept an eye on the door while toggling the dial of Chel's own small HAM that sat at the end of the shop's counter. Even though they now had a working portable, getting the woman onto their frequency was probably wise, at least for the evening.

"Me too," Marisha said, solemnly. The reflective quiet that started to settle over the room was suddenly disrupted by the opening of the front door. Contrary to Derby's concerns, Ruse was not the Gamble sibling that walked into the shop. It was

Natalia, wearing a long coat that obscured her figure and a deep hood that shrouded her face. The outfit was rather effective camouflage. She was shadowed, as always, by Simmons, who blended in a little less fluently, mostly due to his abnormal size. The man still managed a passable disguise, however, covered by a ragged sweater and a dirty hat, the kind you would wear to stave off the cold. Despite the shabby outfit he still wore his fine, wire-rimmed glasses.

Natalia Gamble lowered her hood, letting her hair fall free, and looked around the room. "Marisha, Mr. O'Malley." She smiled at Chel. "I—"

"Swear that you didn't know," Marisha commanded, stepping toward and crowding the much smaller woman while bringing her hand to the weapon that was tucked into her belt.

Natalia didn't need to turn around to know that, behind her, Simmons was reflexively going for his own pistol. The youngest Gamble stood her ground and waved her bodyguard off.

"I had no idea, Maman. I swear it." Her words sounded genuine. "Ruse has shut me out of everything he's been doing since Cain vanished." The youngest Gamble looked away. "I've barely spoken with him in the last couple months." She turned to Derby who stood behind the counter. "That night at the cemetery last week was the only thing he's let me anywhere near recently. I didn't know what he planned to do to King. To any of you."

"It's true, madam," Simmons spoke up, "Ruse has changed. I fear he's become a danger, not only to himself, but, obviously, to those around him as well, including Miss Natalia."

Marisha considered the two of them for a moment then stepped back, giving Natalia space again and easing the tension in the room slightly. "What happened to Cain?' she asked.

Natalia's eyes sank. "I don't know. He's alive," she said, a hint of uncertainty wavering in her voice. "I'm sure he is. Ruse said he abandoned us, fled for The Uppers." She scoffed. "I refuse to believe that." Natalia's gaze floated over to Derby and then back to Marisha. "That's why I'm here tonight. I need to find him. I need to find my brother. This is going to sound strange but. . .I think we might find answers at Gamble House."

Marisha hesitated momentarily, then shook her head. "That doesn't sound strange at all." She walked over to the counter and spread the photos they had found at Notch's apartment across the surface.

Natalia picked up one of the pictures and examined it. "Where did you get these?"

"Off Donovan Notch's dead body," Marisha replied.

Natalia looked up, confused. "Notch? From The Black Ashes?"

"Formerly," Marisha said. "I think he was working with King. Investigating Ruse. I guess Notch had been snooping around Gamble House." She gestured to the photos. "We found this as well." She tossed the small black card onto the counter, the white, block letters standing out starkly. Natalia picked it up.

"Any idea what that is?" Marisha asked.

"Maybe," Natalia answered. "I've seen one before, in Cain's office a few months back. It had something to do with a business deal him and Ruse were fighting about." She put the card back down, shaking her head. "It must be connected but I don't know how."

"Then I guess we'll have to go find out," Marisha said.

Natalia nodded. "I can get us into Gamble House, but it has to be tonight." She looked around at the group. "Whatever Ruse has been planning, it's happening tomorrow."

"Tomorrow?" Derby asked.

The woman nodded.

"Tomorrow is Tithe," Aunt Chel said.

Marisha started, "You don't think. . .The Fifth?"

"I don't know," Natalia replied. "If his ego was big enough to suggest it then, he'd feel even more empowered to act now. Regardless, he's taking almost the entire crew with him tonight, they're heading outside the city to the south for some sort of demonstration. This might be the only chance we'll have to get in there quietly." Marisha looked hesitant.

"Maman, if I was gonna lead you into a trap, you'd be standing in it right now," Natalia said.

Marisha met the Gamble sister's eyes and breathed a deep sigh. "Well, let's get moving then." She nodded to Derby, who removed the radio from his belt, held down the button, and spoke only one word:

"King."

It was a long trip through the dark and up the hill to Gamble House. Despite many years of disrepair, the sprawling, gothic architecture of the facility still cast an intimidating figure over The Reeds, a faded memory of the Gamble family's goodwill.

JT and the Taylor twins had responded to Derby's signal swiftly and met the group in The Drum. From there, the group had headed straight for the outskirts of the city, keeping as much as possible to the alleys and shadows along the way, eventually making it to the hills in the north. The hulking silhouette of the abandoned hospital now loomed over them as they climbed up the sloping path, past the cemetery where all this had started. A time that now felt to Derby, like another life.

As night grew deeper in the sky above, The Bad Moon Crew, plus Natalia Gamble and Simmons, approached a juncture in the dirt road. If they continued straight ahead, up the hill, it would eventually bring them to the foot of the sheer cliff face that separated them from The Uppers. There, they would find a clear, flat area that served as a boarding platform for the huge glass lift that ascended into the unknown world above. Instead, they turned down an even smaller, dustier road to the west which led them into a dense greenbelt covering the hillside surrounding Gamble House.

As they continued toward their destination, venturing further into the thicket, moonlight poked through the spaces in the canopy above them, sparsely lighting their way.

"It's funny," Doc said, scanning the brush around them as they walked.

"What's that?" Derby asked.

"All this green, crowded up here on the hill. It gets thicker the closer to the cliffs you get." Her eyes wandered to the north where you could see the jagged face of the rocky wall in the distance through gaps in the foliage. The impressive shape of The Hydro nestled way above them on the outskirts of The Uppers, peeked out over the edge of the plateau. "I've heard that up at the top they have whole forests."

"They probably have a lot up there that we don't," Derby replied. As they walked, the trees on the left side of the path began to thin, and a view of the city below presented itself. The greenbelt that they were traveling through, spread out down the hill, continuing until just above the cemetery below, where it began to wane and then very quickly faded entirely, giving way to the familiar dust and dirt that blew down into the city proper.

Doc stopped, taking in the view, and Derby stopped beside her, allowing the others to pull ahead. From this vantage, all Derby could see was a pit. The insatiable pit that was Reed City, a black hole at its center, keeping all the things it was waiting to devour in its orbit.

"It's like the green is crawling away from the city," Doc said. "Like even the trees know better."

Derby smiled. "I think they do. That's not a place where things can grow." They spent a few more moments looking out then continued down the path, not wanting to let the others get too far ahead.

"You think she'll betray us?" Doc asked, nodding toward the front of the group where Natalia Gamble walked, in hushed conversation with Marv. The trees had closed around them again, restoring the dim, moonlit ambience to the path.

Derby thought for a moment. "No. But I've never been the best judge of that sort of thing."

Doc chuckled. "Nah, I don't think she will either. She's

nothing like Ruse. Never has been. Besides, she'd never do that to *him.*" She nodded again to the pair at the front. "They can avoid it all they want but some people just. . .fit."

They walked for a short while longer before the trees began to thin on all sides, eventually disappearing abruptly. A clearing had opened up in front of them with Gamble House at its center. The building was impressive, no doubt, but it seemed smaller up close. As if it was the idea of the place that held significance. Across the clearing, a tall, black iron gate guarded a gap in the rustic brick wall that surrounded the whole facility. There were no signs of activity near the entrance, at least as far as they could see, but Natalia led the group along the tree line and around to the side of the building.

After they had made it about halfway down the depth of the facility, the group followed Natalia's signal, darting across the clearing toward the outer wall. It was too tall for any of them to climb alone, so Marv and Doc put their backs to the brick and boosted Natalia up first, who disappeared deftly over the top. The rest of the crew followed suit, one by one, until only the Taylor twins remained on the outside of the wall.

Derby dropped down to the ground inside and found himself at the edge of a large courtyard, dotted with spots of dense and untamed greenery that looked to be slowly consuming a collection of stubby concrete walls, old statues, and winding brick pathways. At the other end of the overgrown yard was a shallow ramp, flanked by steel railings, that led up to a side entrance into Gamble House.

Marv appeared at the top of the wall where he paused, reaching back over and lifting his sister up to join him. They both landed softly on the lawn behind Derby. The group made their way briskly through the courtyard and up the ramp toward the heavy door.

"You think the place is empty, Nat?" Marisha asked.

"Probably not entirely," she replied.

Simmons turned to the group. "It's likely we'll meet *some* level of resistance, especially if this place is as important as we've theorized. We do know that the bulk of our associates have accompanied Ruse to the south, though we do not know for how long." He paused as they reached the door. "We should aim to be brief."

The big man pulled a white card out of his jacket pocket and ran it across the nearby scanner. With a loud click, the lock disengaged, the door came free of the frame, and the Bad Moon Crew entered Gamble House.

14
MESSY IT IS

THE BUILDING'S INTERIOR didn't feel as abandoned as the outside promised. Each hallway they walked down and each room they passed was scantly occupied with gear and supplies, just enough to confirm the building wasn't deserted. Only a scattered number of the overhead lights were on, but enough were lit that it was never dark. The place didn't feel fully forgotten, but it felt temporary.

Most of the space that wasn't empty in the hospital was taken up by big industrial cases, the same ones they had seen coming out of the truck in Notch's photos. Since they weren't exactly sure where to go, these boxes provided a trail of sorts that they followed through the dim halls of Gamble House.

They ventured deeper into the belly of the building, passing many rooms along the way, most of which were unremarkable; a gurney or two, a desk, a stack of boxes; nothing that warranted further exploration. Eventually, the winding corridors led them to a bend, around which they found themselves in a very long, brightly lit hallway. As they moved through the sterile fluorescence, Derby began to hear a faint hum which grew louder the further down the long corridor they crept. Pulling up the rear of the group, Derby was eventually able to identify where the noise was coming from. The low buzz vibrated from the other side of a slightly ajar door near the end of the passage.

The others walked past the door, but Derby stopped, peeking his head cautiously into the room. "Hey!" he hissed down the hall after the rest of the group, then ventured through the door as the others turned around and followed him in.

The source of the hum was immediately clear: a battered-looking generator that rattled away hypnotically in the corner. Aside from the whirring machine, there wasn't much else in the relatively small space; a desk against the far wall, covered in messy stacks of papers, and, on either side of that desk, two huge free-standing tanks. The tanks stood probably ten feet tall, just barely falling short of the room's high ceiling, and were made of a transparent acrylic, through which you could see the murky water that filled each giant cylinder to almost its full height.

"This is. . .weird," Marv said, giving voice to the thoughts of the group as they spread out around the room. Marisha approached the desk and began shuffling through the stacks of loose paper.

"These aren't connected to anything," Derby said, examining the base of one of the tanks. "What are they for?"

"Listen to this," Marisha called out, holding up a sheet of paper which she proceeded to read from:

"Greetings Mr. Gamble,

We are thrilled that you've chosen to sample Renaissance.

By the time this message reaches you, you will have accepted delivery of the equipment required to set up your system. We'll be sending a technician out to the address you've provided, who will install a V3.2 implant in the candidate, as well as hook up your volunteer. Our technician will ensure that everything is in place to provide us with the real-time data collection that we discussed previously.

Additionally, our technician will be fully equipped to field any questions you may have regarding the setup or maintenance of your new system. Volunteer management is usually where we get the most questions and see the most troubles with successful adoption so, please, use this time effectively.

We're very excited to see how Renaissance will transform your business and are looking forward to the beginning of a long and fruitful partnership with The Gamble Family.

Welcome to the inside.
R."

The room was silent as they all processed what Marisha just read. JT was the first to speak. "What the hell is—"

"Shh!" Natalia hissed, bringing the room back to quiet. As they listened, they could hear the very faint patter of footsteps echoing into the room from somewhere in the depths of the facility. After a few moments the footsteps got louder and were accompanied by muffled voices, and after a few more moments, the voices became clear.

"—they're uncomfortable," a woman said. "And I get it, I mean. . .I've heard some strange stuff coming from in there. Heavy breathing and—"

"That's not our business Saf," a man croaked in response. The shadows of the passing speakers darkened the doorway of the room, thankfully only for a moment as they continued down the hall, moving in the direction that the Bad Moons had come from. The hoarse man continued, "We just need to shut up and get through tomorrow. Don't rock the boat." The voices followed the footsteps around the bend, and both sounds faded slowly into silence, leaving the hum of the generator as the sole noise that filled the room once again.

"Jeph and Saffi?" Marv asked.

Marisha nodded. "Ashes must be on guard duty while Ruse is out."

"Well, let's see where they came from then," Natalia said, leading the group out of the room and back into the sterile hallway. On his way out, Derby shot one last glance back into the room at the strange tanks and the murky water that stilled inside them.

They didn't have to travel much deeper into Gamble House to find what they were looking for. Approaching an elbow at the end of another well-lit corridor, they heard the faint muttering of voices. Peeking down the next hallway revealed the owners of these voices to be two members of The Black Ashes, easily identified, even from a distance, by their matching black suits. These two men were standing in front of a large set of double doors about halfway down the hall. If there was something in this building that Ruse was protecting, there was a good chance it was behind those doors.

Before anyone could begin discussing a plan, Simmons removed the shabby hat he had been wearing and fixed his hair. Even though he still had on an unusual outfit, the way he carried himself down the hallway allowed the man to somehow regain his usual, distinguished aura. Without speaking a word, Simmons strolled around the bend and approached the men, carrying with him an air that he was exactly where he was supposed to be. The Ashes guarding the door seemed a bit confused but were not overly alarmed, they knew who Simmons was.

From around the corner, Derby was able to see the man towering over the guards, discussing something with them as he got closer. One of the men chuckled a little as Simmons made a gesture. Then, with an uncanny speed, before Derby could really register what was happening, Simmons incapacitated both Ashes and swept their unconscious bodies to the side of the doors. As soon as this was done the group ran to the previously guarded entrance, Marv patting the big man on the back as they arrived. "Very impressive," he winked.

Marisha pulled on the doors but, unsurprisingly, they were locked, and there was no keypad in sight for them to try their access card on. Acting quickly, Doc pulled out one of her pistols and took off her hoodie, wrapping it around the muzzle of the weapon. She aimed carefully and fired a round into the door, just beside the handle, and then one more on the other side.

Despite the girl's makeshift silencer, the shots still rang out, loud enough to cause the group to look over their shoulders. Marv moved in front of the doors and drove his boot into the wood, causing one of the handles to rattle free and fall to the floor. He landed one more heavy kick, and the doors swung open with a loud creak, revealing a room that was even brighter than the hallway outside. In the center of that brightness, lying on a gurney, with a countless number of tubes and other implements invading his body, was Cain Gamble.

Natalia ran to her brother. Despite its size, the room felt cramped by the sea of machines and equipment that crowded the space.

"Oh God, Cain!" She tried shaking the elder Gamble alert,

but he was completely unresponsive. Derby might have been overwhelmed or disoriented by the many screens and blinking lights all around, but instead, he found his focus fell solely to the man at the center of it all. Cain Gamble's eyelids were wide open but in place of the radiant blue that usually looked outward, the entirety of each of the man's eyes was overtaken by a strange, milky whiteness. An oxygen mask was fixed tight around his face, and his shaved, bare body was assaulted on all fronts by lines of tubing and cable that connected him to the devices that lined the room. The most prominent of these connections was a thick cable, fist-sized in diameter, that ran from the top of his spine into a towering machine behind him that was covered in flashing green dots. The huge presence of the man that Derby met at The Hollow those months ago was not here in this room. The lump of flesh that lay on the gurney had been fully dehumanized, reduced to an instrument, just another piece of equipment.

"Jesus. . ." Marisha and the others were aghast at the scene that was laid out in front of them. "Is he alive?"

"Yes," Natalia replied, her fingers feeling for a pulse in the man's wrist. "We need to get him out of here."

"Nat," Marv said, "we don't know what any of this is." He gestured around the room. "He's alive. . .but for all we know, this stuff is keeping him that way."

Natalia looked at Marv desperately. "We can't leave him like *this.*"

The Soulman nodded, looking around the room. "Yeah." He walked into the nest of machines and began investigating.

"Sim, pull the truck around to the courtyard, we'll meet you there," the youngest Gamble said, tossing her bodyguard a set of keys and crouching down to begin inspecting the primary machine that Cain was hooked up to.

"You have a truck?" Doc asked.

Simmons poked his head out of the doors, surveying the hall outside. "We prepared for the instance in which we may need to leave. . .expeditiously."

"We don't know how many Ashes there are in here, you start driving a truck around, you're gonna draw some attention," Doc said, joining Simmons at the door.

"Can you get him to the yard, Nat?" Marisha asked.

"We're good, Maman. Just get the truck," Marv replied from behind the wall of equipment.

Simmons ventured out into the winding halls of Gamble House followed by Marisha and JT. Doc stopped short on her way out. "Sticks, you coming?"

Derby hadn't taken his eyes off the man on the gurney since they had entered the room. "I'll catch up," he said absently.

Doc hesitated, but let herself leave, following the others to secure their way out.

The milky white of the man's eyes had Derby transfixed. It was as if everything happening around them was tangential. Of less importance. Those eyes were the center, and everything else was just a swirl of noise in their orbit. Derby felt himself being pulled by the immense gravity of the white orbs, inching closer and closer until he bumped into the gurney, which jolted him back to his surroundings.

He looked around the room and could see Marv and Natalia crouched behind one of the big machines, one that had a large screen on the front. The pair were muttering to each other in French, frantically sifting through a nest of wires. He opened his mouth to ask what he could do to help when something clamped down hard on his forearm. Cain Gamble had soundlessly reached up and grabbed Derby; his pale, bare head turned and centered the frosted white of his eyes on the young man. Derby could do nothing except meet the man's empty gaze; his white eyes growing larger and larger, until they enveloped everything, and it was all blank.

The white went on endlessly, in all directions. There was no beginning and no end. Only absence. What could've been an eternity passed, before the formless void began to blur. Only very slightly, but the white started to distort in a way that revealed the faint edges of a shape. Before Derby could make out what it was, it all evaporated.

Derby gasped shooting upright, panting for air. He was on the floor next to the gurney with Marv crouching over him.

"Easy, Sticks. Easy." The Soulman steadied him and helped him to his feet. Cain Gamble looked exactly as he had when they first entered the room, lying limp on the bed, staring blankly at the ceiling. Derby looked down at his arm where the man had grabbed him and found no mark or bruising there.

"You okay?" Marv asked.

Derby nodded, his breathing easing back to a normal rhythm.

"I know it's a lot. All of this. But I need you to steady up for me Sticks. Just till we get out of here. Yeah?"

Derby shook his head, rattling away the cobwebs. "Sorry. I'm good now, thanks. How can I help?"

The Soulman walked to the head of the gurney. "I think we might have a shot at getting him out of here alive. It's a dice roll, but. . .*movement*, right?" He winked.

Derby nodded. From where he stood, he could see Natalia,

still crouched behind the tall machine with the screen on the front, tinkering with the thick cable that snaked across the space and connected to Cain's spine.

Marv turned around and began typing on a set of keys that were mounted under the display, which seemed to be eliciting a response on the screen. "Sticks, if you could hold his head still, I'm gonna try to—" *BANG.*

Marv dropped like a bag of bricks to the ground, blood sprinkling the green glow of the display that he had been standing in front of and pooling around his head where the bullet had gone through.

Derby spun around reflexively and found Ruse Gamble in the doorway, smoke still trailing from the end of his pistol. He was flanked by Arthur Rook and another man that he didn't recognize. Derby fought the impulse to turn and look for Natalia; if the woman had managed to maintain her composure and remain hidden among the equipment, he didn't want to give her away.

Derby forced his eyes to stay on Ruse, noticing how rapid his own breathing had become, though his panic was momentarily sidetracked by the realization that the Gamble leader looked terrible. The man's skin was clammy and pale, there was dried blood crusted around his nostrils, and his hand trembled as he lowered the gun, wiping a thick layer of sweat from his brow. As he continued to watch Ruse, Derby felt anger well up inside him, something he hadn't felt in a long time, and the only thing he could think to do was attack.

He reached for the pistol in his belt; all he needed to do was get the shot off before Ruse did, it didn't matter what happened after that. Just as the weapon came free, before he could even start to aim it, he felt a deep burn in his wrist. Arthur Rook had made it over to him with astounding speed and folded the hand that was holding the gun back the wrong way, until it snapped. The pistol fell from Derby's hand and skittered along the floor. He heard a strained noise escape his throat and felt his wrist give, but he barely noticed any pain, continuing to stare at Ruse with gritted teeth.

Ruse closed his eyes and sighed deeply. "Mr. O'Malley. I know the rest of your friends are scurrying around here somewhere. Are you going to tell me where they are?"

Arthur grabbed Derby by his now broken wrist and squeezed hard, sending a heavy wave of torment up his arm causing him to cry out and drop to one knee, but he managed to maintain defiant eye contact with Ruse. The man shrugged. "Fine. We'll go find them together." Arthur lifted Derby to his feet by the back of his sweater and shoved him toward the door.

They ventured out into the winding halls of Gamble House, Arthur roughly shepherding Derby along as they went. They stopped in a few rooms throughout the facility where the man that he didn't know would perform a quick once over of the space before they'd move along again.

Throughout this whole ordeal, Derby was as numb to his surroundings as he was to the deepening pain in his wrist. Most of what was happening around him only registered as white noise, his thoughts fully hijacked by anger and grief. When they stopped to inspect the room that the Bad Moons had found earlier, the one with the strange, hulking tanks, he barely even heard the group of Black Ashes run in from the hallway, frantically yelling something about the courtyard.

Once again, he was shoved along, more quickly this time, all the way back to where they had first entered the building. Derby was forced to exit the facility into the crisp, night air, marched forward by the pressure of Ruse's pistol on the back of his head, all the way to the edge of the platform at the top of the concrete ramp.

Looking out across the courtyard, he saw close to twenty members of the Gambles and Ashes, all had their weapons drawn, including Jeph who stood at the foot of the ramp. Across the yard, on the other side of the maze of overgrown concrete was a sizable, black truck with its engine running. Spread out around the vehicle was the rest of The Bad Moon Crew, Simmons, and Saffi. They all had their weapons at the ready, and Doc had one of her pistols to the side of Saffi's head, and an arm around her neck.

"*Simmons*?" Ruse sounded surprised. "I guess it *would* have to be the two of you," he said exasperatedly.

"Where's Miss Natalia?" Simmons shouted.

"I don't know, but I can't *wait* to find her," Ruse replied with a snarl. "Listen, I would prefer this not to get messy, I'm sure Jeph would like his sister back unharmed, so how about a little trade?"

"Where's Marv?" Doc asked

"Come now, one for one is a pretty good deal, Miss Taylor. Don't get greedy." Ruse sounded tired.

"Where's my brother?" She pushed her pistol firmly against Saffi's head causing the woman to wince.

"Doc, please!" Jeph shouted.

"Miss Taylor, I am not in the mood for this tonight!" Ruse bellowed.

Doc called out to Derby. "Sticks. . .is he. . ."

Derby shook his head slowly, tears beginning to form in the corners of his eyes.

Doc took a deep, ragged breath and set her jaw.

"Fine, messy it is," Ruse said.

BANG. BANG.

Derby saw Doc in the distance, both her pistols drawn, and he felt Ruse's weapon fall behind him, hitting the ground. He turned and saw blood gushing from a gaping hole in the man's hand where a bullet had gone clean through. More interestingly, the second bullet was sitting against the man's brow, perfectly between his eyes, trying to enter his body, but it was being resisted. Ruse's face was red, he was gritting his teeth hard and blood had started to run from his nose and his ears. The spectacle was enhanced by the searing blue glow that shone from the place behind his ear, where his implant was. The Gamble leader let out a grunt and the bullet gave up, falling to the cement, leaving only a black scuff on his brow where it had been fighting to get inside. Derby felt like he was watching these events in slow motion, but only a second or two had passed. And after those few seconds, the courtyard erupted.

A hail of bullets flew in both directions. Derby watched Arthur Rook grab the third man that had accompanied them out of the facility and cover Ruse, escorting his bleeding leader back to the door. Two of the rounds that were flying all around slammed into the other man's back and he fell to the ground just as Arthur and Ruse slipped back into Gamble House.

Wind whipped against Derby's ear as a bullet passed only inches from his head, bringing him fully into the moment. He tossed himself over the railing that flanked the ramp and dropped down into the courtyard below. On his way to get cover behind a nearby concrete wall, he heard Jeph's hoarse voice scream out. Glancing over to the center of the courtyard, he saw Saffi fall to the ground. The woman's attempt to get through the crossfire and back to her brother had left her full of holes.

Derby ducked behind the low wall, barely avoiding some stray bullets that whirred overhead and continued to make his way around the outside of the courtyard, circling the chaos, moving between pieces of cover, trying to get to the Bad Moons and the big truck.

As he crept along, nearing the opposite end of the yard, a Gamble crew member burst onto the path in front of him, looking for an angle on the Bad Moons' position. With no weapon and a shattered wrist, there was only so much he could do, but he had to do at least that, so he ran full tilt into the man sending them both tumbling to the bricks.

The impact sent a deep wave of pain up his right arm, which he did his best to suppress for now. Once they were sprawled on the ground, he reached, with his good hand, across the man's body attempting to grab his gun. Derby hoped that the man had been caught off-guard, and he would be able to pry his weapon from him in the confusion. Unfortunately, the man was only minorly disoriented and swatted Derby's hand away easily, kicking him hard in the chest as he scrambled back to his feet. Derby gasped from the impact and the Gamble man raised his gun, but before he could fire, a bullet ripped through his knee causing him to stumble followed by another that slammed into his chest crumpling him completely.

"You good, kid?"

Derby looked up and saw Natalia Gamble standing above him holding out her hand. "Yeah, good," he managed to croak out as she helped him back to his feet. Natalia handed him one of Marv's pistols, holding onto the other one herself, and led them the rest of the way around the courtyard. When they got to the truck, they found Simmons first, crouched behind an old statue and bleeding quite heavily from a bullet wound in his shoulder.

"Miss Natalia!"

"Sim!" She ran to the big man, crouching below the statue as bullets continued to fly overhead.

"I'm fine, miss," Simmons said, wincing as he peeked out to return-fire a few rounds into the chaos. A short way down from the statue, another low, vine-covered wall ran across the remaining length of the courtyard. Marisha and JT were posted up here, taking turns reloading and shooting.

When Marisha saw that Derby and Natalia had arrived, she called out: "Time to go!"

Derby ran to the statue and shot some cover fire into the courtyard, unsure if he was hitting anything, while Natalia loaded the injured Simmons into the backseat of the truck.

From the position in which the truck was parked, the direct angle from the courtyard was blocked by a whole row of concrete statues, which had allowed it to not take much damage so far during the shooting.

"Where's Doc?" Derby called out to Marisha who nodded down to the far end of the wall. Doc had both pistols out and was single handedly keeping that side of the courtyard locked down.

"Get in the truck," Marisha called back. "I'll go get h—"

Before she could finish, Derby was running, crouched, down the length of the wall toward Doc.

"Sticks!"

He heard Marisha call after him but ignored it. As he got closer to Doc's position, he noticed four or five bodies of Gambles and Ashes that had tried to flank her unsuccessfully.

"Doc!" He shouted, but the girl showed no sign that she heard anything, stone-faced, and solely focused on fighting. He started to move closer, but out of the corner of his eye, Derby noticed a woman in a black suit crouched behind a shrub all the way at the back of the yard. She must have managed to slip around undetected. As the woman aimed her gun at the surviving Taylor twin, Derby planted his feet, braced his one functional arm, focused his breathing, and fired. His shot almost missed entirely but the bullet just managed to graze the woman's shoulder, which was enough to cause her to flinch back and cry out. This finally got Doc's attention, and she spun around to find Derby there. Her eyes then shot to where his gun was aiming, and like lightning, she fired two quick shots that found their mark in the Ashes woman's torso.

"Doc, we need to go," he said pleadingly.

The daze of violence that had overtaken her subsided, at least enough, and she followed Derby back up to the truck, turning to fire across the courtyard intermittently as they ran.

By the time the two of them approached, the rest of the group had retreated to the truck, Marisha taking the driver's seat while everybody else piled in.

"Heads down and hold on!" Marisha yelled as she slammed on the gas. The truck tore through the courtyard quickly but was met with a storm of bullets as it did. Glass fell around them like pearlescent rain as all the windows of the vehicle shattered, Marisha trying desperately to navigate while remaining safe. They heard the loud pop of a tire getting hit as they burst out from the courtyard and into the front driveway of the facility.

The big truck barreled down the driveway and slammed, full speed into the black iron gates at the bottom, tearing them right off the hinges and exploding out onto the dirt path. Derby poked his head up now that the hellfire had subsided and looked back into the driveway of Gamble House where he could see many small figures getting into vehicles of their own that were parked there.

"No eyes!" JT called out as they entered the surrounding wooded area.

"Everyone, brace!" Marisha waited a bit longer until there was an opening in the treeline and veered the truck sharply off the hill. The truck was able to handle the off-roading for the most part, taking down a lot of the smaller foliage as they bumped and rocked down the steep slope. As the vehicle barreled up to the other end of the greenbelt Marisha slammed on the brakes, bringing the truck to a jolting stop.

"Out! On foot!"

They all piled out and followed Marisha down the slope toward the cemetery. Derby was amazed that everyone here had made it out in one piece. Aside from his broken wrist and the hole in Simmons' shoulder, it was mostly just cuts and bruises. Though this was barely a consolation at all for what they had, once again, lost.

They slunk in silence around the outside of the cemetery and followed the path down into the city. After what felt like an eternity of creeping through backstreets, the battered group made it to the south side and the rusty building that sat on top of the Bad Moons' hideout. As he helped Doc close the heavy door behind them, pain began to set in for Derby. His wrist throbbed, deep breaths hurt his ribs, and the anger that he had felt at Gamble House began to reorganize itself as guilt. Another person, dead. Around *him.*

Marisha held the hatch open while the rest of the crew climbed into the hideout below. Walking in silence next to Doc, Derby was beginning to feel the guilt settle into his bones when, suddenly, all he saw was the dusty floor of the warehouse barreling toward him.

Where the world was moments ago, there was now only absence. Endless, in all directions. A formless void.

END PART TWO

Part Three

Renaissance

15
THE NOTES THAT AREN'T THERE

SIX MONTHS AGO

SOFT SUNLIGHT wove its way through the thin curtains casting the bedroom in a warm, yellow glow. The smell of food floated through the open door and roused Derby, as it did most mornings, and he lay there bleary-eyed, trying to appreciate the peace of the moment.

From his side of the bed, he could see out the door, down the short hallway, and into the tiny kitchen where Etta was softly humming a tune while conducting her morning ritual. Every day, Etta would make breakfast, and in the evenings, Derby would handle dinner. That was the unspoken arrangement they'd had in place for the last three years. This morning, as he lay there basking in the early glow, Derby closed his eyes and listened to the woman's delicate humming as it resonated down the hall.

It was serene.

Etta wasn't a practiced singer, so her voice would dance around the tune in places, yet somehow, every note was perfect. He spent a few minutes here before his growling stomach nudged him out of bed and into his usual morning motion; getting dressed and ready for the day before heading out into the kitchen.

"Morning," he said, gently kissing Etta on the top of the head, then taking a seat at the table.

The woman smiled. "He's alive," she said, running her fingers through her sunny blonde hair and proceeding to tie it up into a messy bun. The small apartment consisted of only two rooms: the bedroom at the end of the short hallway, and the larger room they were in now, which was divided into a small kitchenette and a larger sitting area where the front door could be found. In the corner of this room was an easel that held a large canvas on which a painting was developing. The unfinished piece was a sea of darker blues and blacks contrasted by swirling yellows and reds, the foundational elements of a city skyline at sunset.

"That one's looking really good," Derby said, nodding toward the canvas.

"Is it?" Etta asked, as she dished scrambled eggs from the sizzling pan onto each of their empty plates. "I'm not sure *what* it is yet."

Derby shrugged. "I like it."

"Thanks, baby." She smiled and kissed him softly. "You talk to my dad yet?" she asked, taking a seat across from him at the table.

Derby shook his head, taking his first bite of food. "I'll talk to him today."

"He'll be happy," she said between bites. "Don't get me wrong, he likes Synthia, but I think he'll feel more confident with you up there." Etta sometimes had a secret in her eyes. When there was some emotion that she didn't want to share with the world around her, she'd tuck it away. It was safe from most, but if you looked closely, and you knew her well enough, you could see it there, right where the green in her eyes met the white. Over the years, Derby had gotten pretty good at spotting that secret emotion, and right now he was looking at a spark of sadness.

"It's only for a few months. You could come with me," Derby said, hopefully.

Etta tilted her head and gave him a knowing look. "Derb, you know I can't leave dad for that long. Especially with you gone. Plus, the clinic. . ." She trailed off and continued to eat.

Derby put his fork down and made eye contact with her across the table. "The Reeds won't fall apart without you, Etta. *I* just might."

Etta smiled, leaned over her plate and kissed him. "Like you said, it's just a few months. You'll be fine." Derby nodded and picked his fork back up.

"Also, people have literally fallen apart without me," Etta said, making them both laugh. "Seriously, like detached fingers and shit." Derby chuckled and checked his watch.

"Damn, I gotta go." He stood abruptly and headed for the front door, hastily slipping his shoes on.

"Remember, you're meeting me in The Drum after work tonight," Etta called after him.

"Right. The thing with the people," he said, throwing his backpack over his shoulder and opening the door.

Etta kissed her fingers, gesturing as a chef might when they were satisfied with their work. "Truly, a wordsmith."

Derby laughed on his way out of the apartment. "Love you," he called back, closing the door behind him.

"Oh my word, he's on time." The old man smiled from behind the counter.

"Morning, Otis," Derby said as he entered the small shop.

Otis gestured toward the back of the room. "Fresh aprons in the back."

The store consisted of four narrow aisles separated by tall wooden shelves that held all manner of everyday necessities. Just past these aisles, at the back of the room, there was a shallow closet where Derby dropped his bag and grabbed a clean white apron from a hanger. Otis had moved from the counter to the front aisle of the store where he had begun loading canned food onto the shelves, sitting himself on top of an overturned wooden crate. Derby tied the apron around his waist and headed for the adjacent aisle.

"Where's Synthia?" Derby asked.

"Just us today," the old man replied from the other side of the shelf. "Synth is still a little under the weather."

Derby started loading his side of the shelf with cans from a box that had already been placed at the end of the aisle.

"Did you get a chance to talk with Etta about the Market Exchange?" Otis asked.

"I did."

"And?"

Derby smiled. "She was supportive of it."

"'Course she was," the old man said smiling. "Cain

Gamble's saying we might be gettin' started up there early as next month. You excited?"

Derby grabbed a can from the box, placing it on the shelf. "I still can't imagine what use they would have for our goods in The Uppers but just getting to *see* what it's like up there. . .yeah, I'm excited." Derby paused. "Or at least I was."

He walked to the end of the aisle and rounded the wooden frame to Otis' side, leaning against the shelf and turning a can over idly in his hands. "How disappointed would you be if I didn't go?"

Otis looked at him surprised. "Oh. . .not at all. There was never any pressure. Synthia will be happy to go, and she'll do great up there. If you'd rather stay, don't worry about it, Derby." The old man smiled kindly.

Derby nodded. "I think I do wanna stay"

"That settles it then. To be honest, I'll be a bit relieved to have you here over the summer." Otis chuckled.

Derby smiled. "The plan today was to let you know that I was eager to go. I'm not sure what changed honestly. I really *was* excited, I just," he shook his head, "I don't know. But thank you, for understanding."

Otis shook his head. "It's okay, kiddo. I get it."

Derby turned to head back down his aisle.

"She was such an unruly child, little Etta," the old man said, continuing to load the shelf.

Derby turned back to listen, still rolling the can around in his hands.

"Always getting into trouble." Otis laughed. "Good trouble though, the kind that changed things. After her mother passed, and it was just the two of us, that little girl was the source of all the sweetness in my life." He paused and looked at Derby. "I get it."

KNOCK. KNOCK.

Derby jumped, slightly startled by the sharp rap on the glass door of the shop.

"Is it that time already?" Otis asked, checking his watch.

Derby walked to the entrance, unlocked the door, and held it open for the portly man who had knocked. "Morning, Mr. Binn. On the dot, as usual." The man didn't seem interested in the banter. As he let the door fall closed behind the customer, Derby turned the sign that hung on the inside of the glass so that the side reading OPEN faced outward, welcoming the patrons of Paisley Street.

Derby didn't spend much time in The Drum these days,

but he had never once missed Feast. The affair took place twice a year: once now, as the weather began to turn warm, and again later in the year when a chill crept back into the air. Growing up, attending Feast had been a necessity for him, but in recent years his life had stabilized to the point where he no longer needed to fight for his food. At least no more so than the average resident of The Reeds. He owed a lot of that to Etta.

The bustle bled out from The Drum and down the many arterial streets and alleys at its peripheral, and the smell followed. The alleys just outside of the main rotunda were lined with temporary stands serving a diverse array of home-brewed snack foods. These stands were mostly run by the local shopkeepers and their families who used it as an opportunity to advertise their unique offerings. The main attraction, however, was located at the very center of The Drum itself. A massive ring of serving tables that encircled a modest cooking setup. This area was staffed by volunteers, most of them from the various local crews, and they would spend the evening buzzing around in this ring, churning out hot meals for the huge crowd.

Derby slowly waded through the masses, into the main rotunda, and headed toward the southeast side, where Etta's clinic was. When he was younger, Derby had often wondered how Feast never erupted into chaos. With such a huge concentration of people, and the amount of food being served, it should've been a recipe for disaster. But once he got a bit older, he understood. While the event did indeed host a large congregation of regular citizens, it also demanded a heavy presence of the most prominent groups in The Reeds. The Gamble Family, The Black Ashes, and the whole roster of smaller, lesser-known crews were out in full force, most of them having provided much of the food and resources for the occasion. Causing a scene here could only be the result of a dire lapse in judgement.

"Derb! Here!" Etta waved from a table out front the clinic where she was sitting with a few of her colleagues. Derby joined them, introducing himself to the people he hadn't met before, and greeting the ones he knew. He quickly fell into the atmosphere of the event, not feeling out of place or overwhelmed, like he usually would in this type of situation. He owed that to her too.

After a while, as the rest of their group had begun to mingle into the surrounding crowd, Derby and Etta found themselves alone at the table.

She looked at him, taking a sip of her drink. "Hey, did you chat to my dad today?" she asked.

Derby nodded, taking a swig from his own glass.

"Was he happy?"

"I think so," he replied with a short smile. "I'm not going."

"What?" Etta looked confused.

“I told your dad that I wanna stay here. He seemed okay with it. He’s gonna send Synthia instead.”

“Oh. That’s. . .good, but why, Derb? I thought you were really excited for this?”

Derby waved the idea away. “The Uppers is overrated.” He chuckled. “I dunno it just didn’t feel right I guess.” He took another swig of his drink. “Besides, there’s no *you* up there.”

Etta looked at him, and he saw love. It held the same shape that it did the first time they met. She leaned over, ruffled his short, sandy hair and kissed him. “Well, I guess I’ll have to cancel all the parties I had planned then,” she said, making them both laugh. “Should we brave the mob and get some food?”

He nodded and stood. Etta stumbled as she was getting up and Derby reached out to balance her. “You okay?”

She was shaking intensely as she reached out and stabilized herself against his arm, “I’m fine,” she said looking up at him. As she did, he noticed blood running from her nose.

“Etta, your. . .” he gestured to her nose, and she brought her sleeve up, wiping the red away.

“I’m fine, Derby. I just need a minute.” She stood there taking deep breaths, dabbing her nose with her sleeve intermittently to catch any fresh blood. The shaking gradually calmed down and the bleeding stopped.

"That's the second time now, you need to go see—"

"I will," Etta said. "It's probably nothing. Just stress." She looked him in the eyes. "I'm gonna be fine, okay? We're gonna be fine."

Etta sometimes had a secret in her eyes. A hidden truth she didn't want to share with the world. As always, Derby could see it, the feeling she'd never give voice to. This time, it was something he almost never found there. It was doubt.

FOUR MONTHS AGO

Derby couldn't do it.

He'd been sitting against the cold iron bars of the cemetery fence since before the sun had gone down and given way to the muggy heat of the night. During his repeated attempts at summoning the courage to enter the grounds, he found there was nothing there to muster. The place he was trying to pull the will from was empty. Like every other part of him.

He sat there in the soft dirt, feeling more and more like a husk in the growing darkness. So gripped by his thoughts he barely noticed the voices that echoed up the path or the two figures that accompanied them as they approached the cemetery gates and settled just outside them.

"You okay, brother?"

The smooth voice dragged Derby into awareness. The man who spoke was tall and slim, standing a few feet away, wearing a long dark trench coat over top of a dark hoodie. Beside him was a shorter woman smoking a cigarette and wearing a similar outfit. Both individuals had wild hair that fought to be free of their drawn hoods. Derby couldn't think of how to possibly answer the man's question, so he just stared at them blankly for a few moments.

The tall man nodded. "Sounds about right."

The man turned back to his companion, and they began to speak quietly about something. Derby watched as they stood there, talking amongst themselves, passing the cigarette back and forth. They appeared to be waiting for something.

After some time had passed, a black passenger van pulled up along the dirt path and stopped out front of the graveyard, next to the smoking pair. The driver-side window rolled down slowly but it was too dark to see inside the vehicle. The tall man took something from the inside of his jacket and passed it through into the shadowed interior of the van. After a second, the window rolled back up, and the van drove off.

The woman threw the cigarette into the dirt, stomping it out with her boot, and the two of them began to walk away, down the path toward the city.

“I missed it.” Derby called after them.

They stopped, eyeing him curiously, and then took a few steps back his way. “What’s that?” the man asked.

“Her funeral.” He gestured to the cemetery behind him. “I missed it. I couldn’t—” He paused. “I can’t even go in there.” Derby looked up at them as they inched their way closer. “Have you ever watched someone just. . .deteriorate in front of you?”

The pair looked hesitantly at each other. “I think we’re watching that right now,” the woman said.

“Sorry,” Derby said with a hollow smile. “I don’t know what I’m doing, I. . .”

“I’m Marv,” the man said gently. “This is my sister, Doc.” The woman nodded slightly. As the man gestured to his sister, Derby noticed a tattoo on the back of his hand, the dark shape of a vinyl record.

“Derby,” he replied.

“Sorry for your loss, Derby,” Doc said as the siblings sat down against the fence on either side of him. “What was her name?” she asked.

Derby breathed deeply. “Etta.”

“That’s a nice name,” Doc said, smiling. “What was she like?”

“Ah.” Tears started to well in his eyes. “She was. . .everything.

She was kind and ambitious. Loving and protective. She was one of those people that, when she was around, everything felt okay somehow." He blinked, sending a stream rolling down his cheeks. "She made you feel like you meant something." He sighed and wiped his eyes with his sleeve. "She was a terrible singer."

The siblings chuckled.

"But even that was perfect somehow. I can't imagine never hearing her again."

"Mm," Marv said. "See, that's the thing about music, Derby. It's just as much about the quiet parts. The pauses and holds. Those are essential to the piece. So, maybe that's where you'll find her now, in the spaces between. In the notes that aren't there. But trust me, brother, she's still a part of the song."

Derby nodded.

The three of them sat quietly in the stillness of the night for a few moments.

"What are you gonna do now?" Doc asked.

Derby shook his head. "I have no idea."

Marv looked at him thinking for a moment before speaking. "Why don't you hang with us for a bit? Come meet the rest of the crew."

"You guys have a crew?" Derby asked.

Doc shot a questioning look across to her brother who dismissed her concern with his eyes.

Marv stood, brushing off his pants. "It ain't much, but it might be better than sitting out here alone." Doc followed suit, hopping up to her feet.

Derby sat there looking up at the high cliff upon which The Uppers was perched. "I dunno, I think I just need to get the hell away from here. Maybe up there, start fresh." He nodded toward that higher place, where the bulky silhouette of The Hydro loomed large, inviting him to wonder what lay beyond it.

"Hah. Well, I can't promise you we'll get ya to The Uppers, but we can get you off the ground, I'm confident," Marv said.

Doc reached her hand out toward Derby who sat there for a long moment. Finally, he took the woman's hand, pulled himself up off of the dirt, and followed the siblings, who, only minutes ago were strangers, down the path toward The Reeds, leaving the shadow of the cemetery behind.

16
WHAT HAPPENS TO US

THE VASTNESS OF *the void created a claustrophobic feeling in Derby. As if the further the emptiness expanded, the more his awareness was forced to shrink. This place was not a dream. He wasn't sure how he knew that so certainly, but he was really here, at least in all the ways that mattered. The total absence of this place wasn't only material, but a complete starvation of the senses as well. The omission of everything made it impossible to have any grasp of time, but eventually, just like when he found himself here before, something started to materialize. The white began to blur, only slightly, but enough for a shape to emerge. The faintest outline of a tall box developed in the space in front of Derby, accompanied by a hazy pink that tinted the white around the edges. Then suddenly, again, he was pulled away.*

"Whoa, hey. You're okay, dude."

Derby found himself sitting upright on a mattress in the Bad Moon den, chest heaving. Doc and JT knelt on either side of him and Marisha stood at the foot of the mattress, a look of desperate relief on her face.

"You're okay, right? You hit the floor pretty hard." Doc said.

He scooted himself back, so he was sitting against the dirty wall and nodded, closing his eyes. "I'm good. I just need a minute." As his breathing slowed back to a normal rate, Derby's eyes wandered to the corner of the hideout where Natalia was tending to Simmons' shoulder wound.

"The Fifth *must* be his target. At Tithe tomorrow," the youngest Gamble sibling said as she pulled tight the makeshift bandage she'd been wrapping around her keeper's bare upper body. She stood, turning to Marisha. "The Drum is our best bet. Getting to them on that stage, in front of everyone? That's his move. We'll have to setup around—"

"Natalia." Marisha looked calmly at the woman. "What are we going to do?"

"What do you mean, Maman? We're going to stop him," Natalia said matter-of-factly.

"How? He has the numbers, *and* he's got. . .whatever

Renaissance is." Marisha shook her head. "I can't lose any more people, Nat. I'm sorry."

Natalia looked angry. "You can't just—"

"It doesn't matter, Marisha," JT interjected. "What happens to us. It doesn't matter. Not anymore."

Marisha looked momentarily defiant, then, stepping back slowly, the woman dropped to the ground, leaning against the thick wooden leg of the table in the center of the hovel, and began to weep.

JT stood and walked over to Marisha, kneeling beside her. The girl removed the carved wooden necklace from around her own neck, the last memento she had of King and hung the keepsake around Marisha's shaking shoulders. The Bad Moon leader looked down, recognizing the carving, and met the young girl's gaze.

"We do this for them," JT said, touching the wood that now lay against Marisha's chest. "We don't let him get away with this."

Natalia sat down next to Simmons, leaning her head back against the wall and the room was still for a while.

Pain crept back into Derby's body. His right wrist had puffed up and started to turn a dark shade of blue; every motion he tried to make with it sent a shock of hurt up his arm. His eyes fell on Doc who was still next to him, looking off into the corner of the room. She looked hollow. The playfulness that usually wound its way through the angles of her face was no longer there.

Suddenly, he remembered something.

"It hurts him." Everyone in the room turned to look at Derby. "Or. . .something. It takes a toll on him, using Renaissance. He looked like shit at Gamble House. He was bleeding and barely able to stop your bullet." He nodded toward Doc. "He must have been using it before he got there." Derby winced, adjusting his wrist.

JT walked over to where Natalia was sitting, grabbed the sheet of white fabric that she had been using to bandage Simmons, and brought it over to Derby. She began wrapping his wrist, inserting two tightly rolled pieces of fabric on either side of the joint, building a makeshift splint. Deep bruising had set in around the young girl's eyes from her broken nose, the one she had received while saving his life. Even after all the pain he'd brought into her world, here she was, helping him.

"If it takes something from him physically, to use it, that means he's got a gas tank," Natalia said.

Doc jumped in. "Which means we can let him make his big play and then hit him when he's low."

The group's eyes collectively fell on Marisha, waiting for her to weigh in. The woman braced on her knees, pushing herself to her feet. "We're sprinting uphill here. . .but shit, we always have been. And knowing that he'll be on a clock helps." She looked around the room at the battered crew and shook her head, tucking the wooden necklace under her shirt. "Fuck it. Even if we can't stop the bastard, at least we can make it difficult for him. We'll setup in The Drum tomorrow, get some sleep if you can."

JT finished setting Derby's wrist and then joined the others in finding a piece of mattress to curl up on.

Derby shifted himself flat, his whole body radiating with pain. He stared across the room feeling simultaneously awake and exhausted and found himself focused on the small black letters that stood out against the yellow panel of the strange cabinet. The letters were thin, he noticed; like whoever wrote them was rationing their ink. He felt the same way.

Why had he fainted again? At Gamble House he figured it had just been too much. The weight of the situation they were in, the dehumanized state of Cain Gamble, all of it. Maybe this was his body's way of telling him he was in over his head. Just as he began to doubt that any of them would truly get to sleep that night, the yellow of the cabinet disappeared as his eyes fell closed like anvils and he drifted into darkness.

"What do *you* need?"

Etta sat across from him, the same way she had every morning when she was alive. Her blonde hair tied up in a hurried bun, her striking green eyes looking straight into him. This *was* a dream. The murky haze that obscured their surroundings confirmed that. In this dream, the person sitting across from him was Etta in form, but the voice that came out of her mouth and the words that she spoke belonged to Cain Gamble.

"Something you don't already have," Etta said in Cain's voice.

These were words he'd heard the eldest Gamble speak the only time he'd met him, before the man's own brother turned him into a husk.

"I don't have a good answer." The words escaped though he did not command them to. He said them now because they'd already been said all those months ago. Those months that felt like millennia. Etta opened her mouth as if to continue but before he could hear what she would say next, what Cain Gamble had said before, the scene around him was disrupted by a sharp pain.

In his sleep, Derby had rolled over onto his broken wrist,

and the pain now slowly pulled him back to the world. As he settled into consciousness, he looked around the room and was surprised to find the rest of the crew asleep. He supposed once the adrenaline and the shock had been tempered, exhaustion was all that remained. He lay there for a while, thinking of Etta. Of how radically his life had transformed when she entered it, and how it did so again when she was ripped away. His thoughts then wandered to King and to Marv and to the way in which the lives of the Bad Moon Crew changed once *he* entered their picture. They'd done nothing but try to help him, and in return he'd brought disaster to their door.

Lurching to his feet, shoes still on from the night before, Derby moved across the room, stepping as softly as he could to avoid waking the others. As he made his way carefully, he thought of where he'd go next and how he would get there. He'd been dragging these people down for long enough. It was time to set them free. To spare them the trouble.

"Leaving?"

Derby jumped, almost falling headfirst into the ladder at the foot of the hatch. He turned and saw Doc sitting at the central table, unsure how he had possibly missed her until then.

"Jesus, Doc," he hissed.

"I don't blame you," she continued in a soft voice, low enough to avoid rousing the rest of the group. "This isn't your stand to make."

Derby walked over to the table, heart rate coming back under control, and quietly pulled out a chair, taking a seat. "It's not that."

The body sling that had belonged to Marv was out on the table, both of his pistols still in it. Natalia must have grabbed it off him on her way out of Gamble House, she had given Derby one of those guns to fight with in the courtyard. Aside from the weapons, there was also a small pouch attached to the sling which Doc reached into, withdrawing a coin, that she then rolled along her fingers.

"What have I done since you guys brought me in, Doc?" Derby asked. "Other than be a liability?" He looked down, shaking his head. "I'm not leaving because I think it's hopeless, I'm leaving so that it isn't."

"Oh, shut up, Sticks. Stop acting like you're some sorta curse." She looked at him for a moment then sighed deeply. "Do what you gotta do."

They sat there for a moment, Doc's eyes fixed on the coin as it travelled hypnotically across her knuckles, the pill tattoo on the back of her hand distorting as her fingers flexed. "It was Marv that came up with the name. 'Sticks'. Last few years we'd made a bit of a habit of bringing new people around. Marv and I had been feeling like we needed to increase our presence a bit. None of them ever lasted. Some got cold feet, but mostly King just wouldn't approve of anyone." She chuckled. "Anyway, a few days into you being here, I was talking about how I didn't think you'd last the week, and Marv looked at me and said '*Betcha a coin this kid sticks.*' She held the coin up in front of Derby. "From the beginning, right from that night at the graveyard, he believed in you." She put the coin down on the table and slid it toward him. "So, do what you gotta do, Sticks."

He sat there for a while, looking at the bronze disc in front of him. Finally, he reached out slowly and slid the coin back across the table, looking her in the eyes. "I'm sorry, Doc." He stood, walking to the ladder.

"At least take this then." Doc pulled the portable radio off her belt and handed it to him.

"I can't, I—"

She thrust it into his hand and forced his fingers closed around it. "We're not gonna need it. Besides, if by some miracle we survive tomorrow, and by an even bigger miracle you manage to pull your head out of your ass," she gestured to the radio, "7.15. You always have a place here, Derby. For a day or a decade."

He nodded, clipping the radio to his belt. "Thank you, for everything."

She smiled faintly.

Derby took a deep breath and climbed the ladder, exiting

the den through the hatch and leaving behind what was left of the Bad Moon Crew.

17
THE ENGINE OF PROSPERITY

DERBY DIDN'T HAVE a plan, but the unseasonable warmth of the day made that slightly more tolerable. Maybe he'd go south. He'd never been past the southern limits of The Reeds and had never known anyone who had. Maybe it was better there. Or maybe it was worse.

The streets were buzzing as the city got ready for Tithe. Most of the shops were closed but he'd managed to find one on the east side of town that was up and running and had been able to trade his wristwatch for what, by his assessment, was a week's worth of food; a mix of dried and canned, along with a pack to carry it in.

As the morning grew late, Derby found himself in

The Drum, chewing on some dried fruit at a table near the perimeter. He kept his hood up, remembering that he was still technically a wanted man, but there was so much hustle in the city center, preparing the stage and the surrounding area for that afternoon's ceremony, that he'd be shocked if anyone paid him more than a passing glance.

The Tithe ceremony was scheduled to start in the late afternoon, just like it had every other year, giving The Fifth Council a couple hours of daylight to work with. Despite their jovial approach to the festivities, the council members never spent longer than they needed to in The Reeds. The whole event was a mugging masquerading as a celebration. Ruse Gamble was a despicable man, but he wasn't wrong about The Uppers. Over the years, they had bled Reed City dry, and they would continue to do so until there was nothing left.

Derby wasn't sure what his next step was going to be, or if he had made the right choice by leaving the Bad Moons, but he was confident that they'd have better luck stopping Ruse without him around. Especially since it seemed he could no longer rely on his body to work properly. He hadn't fainted since returning to the hideout last night and though he was sure it was just a stress response to everything that had happened, he couldn't be sure it wouldn't happen again. What he was sure of was there was something he needed to do, one of the many things he'd been putting off for too long.

The sun had passed its zenith as Derby trudged up the dirt path north of the city. His pace slowed as he approached the cemetery gates, his eyes drifting to the spot along the fence where he had first met the Taylor twins those few months ago. He pushed open the dark iron gate and entered the graveyard proper. The last time he was here, they had been making a drop to Ruse, and he had received a warning that, in retrospect, he may have done better to heed.

'*Learn your leash.*'

Would it have mattered?

The cemetery stretched out in front of him, directly ahead was the slope up to the lookout where they had met with the Gambles, and off to the left the lawn bowed slightly downwards then opened up wide, dotted with headstones all the way to the distant fence that surrounded the perimeter.

Derby took a deep breath and then walked slowly down to the left, into the sprawling, open patch of cemetery, all the way across to a plot in the back corner that was nestled under a tall tree. He stood there for a long while in silence before finally finding his voice.

"Hey," he said shakily, scanning the area around the grave. "They picked a nice spot." Derby lowered himself to the ground, sitting on the grass. "I don't really know what to say Etta. I guess I'll start with I'm sorry. Sorry it took me so long to come here. Sorry that you're gone. I'm just. . .sorry."

He looked up at the branches of the tree that blocked out the sun above him. While mostly green, some of the leaves had begun to turn color with the season. "I don't know if I'm doing the right thing. Or if there even *is* a right thing to do." His gaze lowered to Etta's headstone. "When you left, I felt somehow responsible. Like I could have done more, like I should have been able to save you. And since then, anything that's reminded me of you just. . ."

He slid his backpack off his shoulders, letting it slump onto the ground beside him, and unclipped the portable radio from his belt, setting it down in the grass. "I feel guilty for avoiding your dad but seeing him would be one of those painful things that I haven't been brave enough to face, I guess. When I met the Bad Moons, it felt like the first step toward a new start. The first step on my way out of this hole, which was the only thing I could imagine doing after you were gone. Leaving The Reeds." Derby held his hand out in front of him and realized it was shaking. He took a deep breath.

"Then that all went to shit. We lost King, then Marv." He shook his head. "This city has done nothing but take from me. My whole life, really. You were my only break from that. Then it took you too." Tears started to well up in Derby's eyes. "So maybe, if I just let everything go, don't hold onto anything, there'll be nothing left for the world to rob me of."

He wiped his eyes with his sleeve, sniffing. "I can't imagine *you'd* ever do that. You'd probably grab onto everything tighter, look the world in the face and scream, '*Take it from me, I dare you.*'" He smiled, letting his eyes drift back to the canopy of leaves above. "I wish you were still here, Etta."

Derby sat there with his thoughts, beside Etta's grave, until eventually, the sun inched to the other side of the tree and beat down on him, battling the otherwise cool air of the afternoon. Derby pushed off the grass and got to his feet.

"Well, I don't know what I'm gonna do next but, I'll come back soon, I won't stay away again. I promise." He turned, reaching down with his good hand and picked up his backpack, slinging it over his shoulders. As he bent down to grab the radio from where he had set it down, Derby was suddenly overcome with a familiar weakness, falling to the soft ground, and feeling consciousness slip away from him.

Doc was starting to sweat from her vantage on the roof of Aunt Chel's shop. The sun was getting lower in the sky, but it still radiated warmth over the parts of the city it touched, despite the crisp air of the turning season. She could see the whole of The Drum from the low rooftop and had a clear view of the stage that stood in the center. The large Tithe container that they had spent months filling with valuables had been moved from the alley beside Chel's into the center of The Drum. The rotunda was packed with people, standing shoulder to shoulder, chest to back, on all sides of the stage, the crowd stretching all the way to the perimeter and spilling deep into the streets and alleys that fed the market. Sunlight glared off the three billboard-sized screens that craned over the square, obscuring the images that flickered there, rendering them ornaments.

As the ceremony neared, Doc checked her person, feeling the double pistols that hung at her sides in the sling that once belonged to her brother; her hands moved on to find the third gun she had strapped to her boot, tightening the belt that held it there and making it snug. Doc was singularly focused. Ruse Gamble had taken everything from her, had left her empty. The world around her felt devoid of meaning and the only substance she could imagine was getting a bullet into that man's head.

A small path had been cleared through the crowd leading out of The Drum to the north, lined by an assembly of A's. The way had been secured to allow the approach of two vehicles and that now rumbled into the square. One small, black car, and a much larger truck with an empty flatbed. The smaller vehicle stopped near the stage while the truck continued, stopping next to the Tithe container.

A host of A's flooded the stage, creating a wall around the edges of the platform and the doors of the small black car opened, allowing the members of The Fifth Council to climb out. They weren't impressive or outlandish figures. As they took the stage, Doc couldn't help but notice how normal they were.

It was easy to exaggerate the idea of people in your mind when they loomed so large over your daily life, but once a year she got a reminder of how small these gods really were. Just people. People that were vulnerable. If Doc wanted to, she could put bullets on them right now. The Fifth were betting that the fear of retribution would be a strong enough deterrent to keep them safe. An arrogant bet, but one that they had always won.

"Hello, Reed City!" One of the members of the Fifth, a tall, thin woman, had begun to address the crowd, speaking into a microphone that projected through a small set of speakers on either side of the stage. "The Fifth Council of Augusta is here today to thank you for your continued support and investment."

Doc scanned The Drum, finding no signs of the Gambles. No Ashes either. She could see Marisha and JT dotted in the crowd, right where they had planned to be. Natalia and Simmons were perched on their own building across the market. She saw no signals from any of her companions yet.

"Another Tithe, another year for our respective cities to flourish." A regiment of men had begun to load the Tithe container into the flatbed of the large truck. "You may wonder what this investment means. Why it's important." The other four members of The Fifth stood attentively in the middle of the stage while the woman speaking paced the perimeter, addressing all sides of the crowd. "This generous contribution, from all of you hardworking citizens, is a direct investment in the future of this booming metropolis. It is fuel for the engine of prosperity. Every bit of material you've given here today," she said, gesturing to the container, "Augusta will commit back into your city tenfold." This was met with timid applause that rippled throughout the crowd.

As the woman continued her speech, Doc grew restless. Ruse had to be making his move soon, but there wasn't even the faintest hint of him yet. She did another scan of her allies, still no signals. Suddenly, she heard the door to Chel's shop slam open below.

"Doc!" Aunt Chel called up to her.

Doc moved, cautiously, to the edge of the roof where she saw the old woman standing below looking frantic.

"Doc, it's the radio. Sticks is on the HAM."

Empty. Endless.

He had been ripped from the cemetery and pulled back to this non-place. To the vast, white nothing.

Derby wasn't sure what was going on, what these episodes were, but he felt an odd sense of calm about it all. It didn't feel dangerous. He stood there in the vacant white until, just like the times before, the void began to blur forming the edges of a shape.

A tall rectangle once again appeared before him, accompanied by a tint of pink where the shape met the emptiness. This time, as the shape matured, it became clear that the shape was a door, and the pink tint around the edges was light shining through the frame.

Derby stepped closer, and the door became more palpable. There was no knob, but there was firmness there, like it was inviting him to push it open. Derby reached out his hand but before he could make contact, the void swirled and gave way to the world once again.

He felt the sun beating down on him as he sat up, breathing heavily and looking around the cemetery. Derby was still alone, as far as he could tell, so he took a few moments, sitting there in the grass, to get his breath under control. It didn't take him long to recover. Once he felt stable, he adjusted the bag on his back and stood, picking up the radio and clipping it onto his belt. As he made his way back toward the entrance, he tried to make sense of what was happening to him.

Distress was how he justified these episodes, his body's way of rebelling, but considering them now, he couldn't help but wonder if it was more than that. They had started with Cain Gamble touching him at Gamble House. Those endless white eyes consuming everything. And every time he awoke he had an itch in the back of his mind. A memory of a place that wasn't a place. And a door.

Derby stopped as he neared the cemetery gates, and his eyes wandered up the slope to the small outcropping at the top where he had received that grim warning from Ruse Gamble. He turned and headed for the outlook.

As he trudged up the hill his thoughts wandered to the Bad Moons and what might be happening back in the city right now. Reaching the top of the hill, he leaned forward on the short wooden fence that surrounded the area, taking in the view of The Reeds. He could see the concentration of bodies in The Drum from here, a dense cluster of dots filling the center of the city. The Tithe ceremony had probably already begun. He wondered if Ruse had made his move yet, if the Bad Moons were all okay, if by removing himself from the equation he'd saved them. What if instead he'd doomed them?

He turned away from the fence, feeling as uncertain now as he had the last time he was up here, being interrogated. His eyes wandered to a nearby grave, the one that the Gambles had dug up that night, and he stomped down the soft slope toward the plot.

As he stood in front of the grave, the image of the Gamble men re-filling the hole flashed in his mind. To think that was only a week ago, and at the time, that was one of the most disturbing things he had ever witnessed. His gaze fell to the headstone and the name inscribed upon it: **DANNY CAHILL.** He started to wonder what Ruse could have possibly wanted with this man's body, when his attention was drawn back to the name. *Danny Cahill.* It was familiar. He didn't know the man, but he'd heard the name.

Suddenly, it hit him. The Uppers facility, the one that Ruse had used Derby to rob. The file he had stolen was a records file for Danny Cahill, Director of Operations at. . .*Reed City Hydro.*

Derby spun, looking up, to the top of the elevator at the edge of The Uppers, where he could see the back side of the hydro facility cresting over the edge of the cliffside. And he remembered Ruse's words to him, last week, not ten feet from where he was standing now. '*We're drinking their shit, son.*'

"Oh my God." The words fell out of Derby's mouth.

He fumbled for the portable radio on his belt and set it to the 7.15 frequency used by the Bad Moons. It was a long shot, but he hoped that maybe someone had stayed behind at the hideout and would hear him.

"Hello! Is anyone there?" he said, holding down the button to transmit. He waited a few seconds with no response.

"Doc? Marisha? JT? Anyone! It's Sticks!"

They were probably all at The Drum, waiting to ambush Ruse, he wouldn't be able to—

BZZT. "Hello? Sticks?"

It was Aunt Chel.

"Chel? Where are you?"

"At the shop, where else would I be?"

She must've left her HAM on 7.15 after he had changed it last night.

"Chel, the Bad Moons are somewhere at Tithe, I need you to get them, I need to talk to them." He started a light run down the slope toward the cemetery gates.

"Doc's on the roof, do you want me to—"

"Yes, Chel, please. I think they've got it wrong. . .Ruse isn't going to The Drum."

18
EVERYTHING FOR THIS

DOC HOPPED DOWN to the street off the low roof of Aunt Chel's shop, turning and following the woman inside. She rushed to the end of the counter and picked up the transmitter attached to the HAM.

"Sticks?"

Derby's voice crackled through the radio. "*Doc! Oh, tha— God. Have you — the Gambles yet?*" The transmission was faint and cutting out.

"No, nothing yet. Sticks, where are you? You're breaking up."

"*Listen, you're — wrong place. I think — I th — Ruse is going to The Hydro.*"

"The Hydro? Why would he. . .Sticks, tell me you're not going there alone."

"*I'm almost — and losing — there —*"

"Sticks!" She waited for a response but only static came through the speakers.

"Dammit." She hurried out of the shop and into the thrum of the crowd. She needed to gather the others and head for The Uppers. They'd need to use Buck's van; if Sticks was right, and he was going there alone. . .

No. She wouldn't lose anyone else.

The radio lost signal completely when he reached the fork in the path that broke off to the west toward Gamble House. Instead of taking the divergent road, Derby continued north up the hill and very quickly found himself fully enveloped by the shadow of the towering cliff.

A little further along, and he was standing at the doors of the glass-enclosed lift. It was massive up close; big enough to fit at least two large vehicles side-by-side. It should've been impossible that anything could move the towering glass structure against the will of gravity, but the sheer weight and ruggedness of the hulking gears and rails around it made the task seem inevitable.

Much to Derby's surprise, the surrounding platform was completely unguarded. He figured he'd at least need an access card to operate the elevator but when he pressed the round button next to the doors, they slid open freely, inviting him on board the glass carriage. Maybe Ruse had drawn the A's away, or maybe anyone could take the ride, but if you weren't intended to be there when you got to the top, you'd never come back down.

Derby tried not to think about that as the doors closed behind him and the lift lurched into motion, beginning to carry him upwards. The structure around him was completely translucent, top to bottom; it felt as if he was floating up the cliffside. This must have offered a staggering view of the city below as he was pulled away from it, but Derby kept his gaze straight ahead, watching only the rock face speeding by outside, a seemingly endless stream of stone.

What if he was wrong? What would be waiting for him topside? What if Ruse had made a deal with the A's to let the Gambles through to The Hydro, then they might still be waiting above. He had no choice but to count on the man's disdain for The Uppers and on his brutality. When the lift finally slowed to a stop and his long trip up the cliff came to an end, the doors slid open, and Derby's hunch was validated.

The outpost that sat outside the elevator doors was a bloody mess. As he stepped off the lift and onto the reception platform, he counted close to fifteen bodies strewn about in various displays of carnage. All had been heavily armed.

"Shit." He couldn't afford to delay. He pressed on across the platform, and followed a wide brick road that led north, further uphill. He hadn't gone far down this path before he crested the hill and was met by the full view of the plateau.

The Uppers.

The scene laid out before him was breathtaking enough to give him pause. The land stretched on in all directions as far as he could see. In the north, the horizon line was shadowed by the silhouette of a forest that spread to the bounds of his vision to both the east and west. The vastness of the land was impressive, but even more so was the city of Augusta, which stood pristine in front of him. The stunning capital sat at the bottom of a shallow, natural bowl that formed in the earth ahead, the ridge on which Derby now stood formed the southern lip of this formation. The city seemed smaller than he had imagined, but the presence of the place was pronounced by its elaborate architecture. Everything was clean glass, marble, and stone. Even though he had high ground on Augusta, the sight of the city made him feel small. As he stood in awe of the untarnished city before him, he noticed his breathing; even the air up here seemed cleaner. More vital.

From where he stood, the brick road that he had followed up from the elevator platform wound forward, a twisting path that led down into the city below. Jutting off from the bricks was a narrow, dusty service road that led along the elevated ridge surrounding Augusta, all the way up to The Hydro. The facility stood tall above the city. The sight of the massive building snapped Derby back into the moment, and he took off along the ridge toward the place where he was now almost certain he'd find the Gambles.

As he ran, heart thumping in his throat, the full scope of the building he was approaching came into view. The piece that was visible from The Reeds was only a fraction of the large industrial complex. The most impressive part of the facility was the massive reservoir that was attached to the main building. A sealed enclosure that ran along the ridge, matching the curve of the bowl formation that held the city below. The reservoir extended almost all the way to the distant north side where the forest was, and was pierced, at various spots along its length, by large pipes that snaked all the way down into the ground beneath Augusta.

As Derby neared the facility, he found the heavy doors of the main entrance wide open, a good sign that he was in the right place. Hopping up the short set of concrete steps, he noticed the keypad beside the doors was flashing between green and red. He ducked into the facility. The entrance was wide and shallow with tunnel-like passages leading off on either side of the room. A single guard lay dead at the desk in a pool of his own blood, his lifeless hand still loosely gripping his pistol. Derby instinctively ran to the desk, grabbed the weapon from the man's corpse, and headed down the tunnel on the right side of the room. He didn't get far down the passage before he began to hear voices which grew louder as he approached a bend in the tunnel, prompting him to slow to a stop so he could peek around the corner.

"You can't be serious!"

Around the bend, the narrow channel opened up into a large circular room that was full of both Gambles and Ashes. There were fifteen or twenty crew members in total, a mix of both groups. The pale, bald leader of The Black Ashes was the source of the raspy shouts that echoed down the hallway. Jeph was standing next to Ruse, who was typing something into a console on the side of the room, as always, flanked by Arthur Rook.

"We gave up everything for this," Jeph croaked. "For independence. That's what you promised Ruse, a fresh start for The Reeds. You didn't say anything about a massacre."

"It's no less than what they've been silently doing to us for years." Ruse looked fully recovered from the fragile state he'd been in last night, though his right hand was wrapped up where Doc had shot him clean through. The man was barely listening to Jeph. He reached into his suit jacket and pulled out a small silver case. It was hard to see from where Derby was, but he was pretty sure Ruse pulled a severed finger out of the box. He proceeded to place the small lump of flesh against a scanner next to the console, causing it to flash green. Something above them grinded loudly in response.

It was only now that Derby noticed two huge pipes that crowned the ceiling of the big room. These massive metal tubes entered through the floor on the opposite side of the circular room from where Derby was, wound their way around the ceiling, and exited right above the passage where he stood.

Jeph looked very distressed, his voice even more ragged than usual. "This is different, there's thousands of people down there. Kids."

Ruse turned, looking directly at the man. "What about *our* kids, Jeph? The ones that starve because there isn't enough to go around." They stared at each other for a moment. Derby looked down using his uninjured hand to make sure the safety was off on the pistol he'd salvaged, and that it was loaded. He closed his eyes and steadied his breathing.

Jeph softly broke the silence, speaking almost in disbelief. "I lost my sister for this."

"And I lost my brother!" Ruse bellowed, walking away from Jeph into the center of the room. "For Christ's sake, Jeph, don't be so naïve." He turned back to the pale man. "This was never gonna be free. It was always gonna cost us *everything*."

BANG.

The bullet found its mark, striking directly at the side of Ruse's head, where it stopped abruptly a few inches from making contact and fell feebly to the ground at his feet. The Gamble leader turned and found Derby who stood, still aiming the weapon at his intended mark.

"Mr. O'Malley?" the man said, an air of respect in his voice. He smirked, casually kicking the fallen bullet aside. "As impressed as I am that you've made it this far," he kept his eyes on Derby as he walked back over to where Jeph was standing, "I don't have time for you right now." Ruse reached out and grabbed Jeph's pistol from the holster on the man's belt and in one swift motion, levelled the weapon directly at Derby and fired.

The flash of the muzzle blinded Derby and he felt his body go limp. Strangely, in that moment, there was a complete absence of pain, and everything faded to white.

Not possible.

Ruse stood, Jeph's pistol still smoking in his hand, staring stunned at the slumped figure of the boy across the room. The bullet he had fired lay loose next to the unconscious body of the O'Malley kid.

It didn't make sense. It looked like Renaissance had deflected that shot. Nothing else could've done that. The kid had gone limp and passed out right as the bullet made contact. Ruse rubbed his temple; he was having trouble thinking straight with Jeph yelling in his ear. He couldn't, for the life of him, identify the words the man was shouting. It was just noise, and he needed quiet. Ruse aimed the pistol behind him, keeping his eyes on the mouth of the tunnel where the boy was.

BANG. BANG.

Jeph stopped shouting.

Ruse vaguely heard the chaos erupt behind him as he walked over to the unconscious body. Immediately, his hands felt around the kid's neck and behind his ears, looking for an implant. There wasn't one. Of course there wasn't, how would that have even been possible? But without an implant, that couldn't have been Renaissance. The futile bullet that lay nearby and the pulse that still throbbed in Derby's neck suggested otherwise.

Ruse let Derby's limp body fall back to the ground and stood, frustrated. He turned back to the disaster that now painted the back side of the room and nodded to Arthur who had ducked behind the console to avoid the carnage. Arthur knew his boss's gestures well and made his way over to the boy, brandishing his short blade. Ruse left the man to his work and walked back over to Jeph's body.

The man lay there, pale as ever, and vacant. His coat had fallen open, and a little silver box had tumbled out onto the floor, revealing the black cigarette that the man always carried. The thing was still lit, a thin trail of dark smoke rising from its tip. The two holes that Ruse put in the man's chest had stopped leaking but the results of the riot they had spurred were all over the room. Well over half of both the Gambles and the Ashes lay dead across the floor, whatever men remained had taken the fighting out of the big open room and into the tunnel; shots and screams could be heard echoing throughout the facility. He tossed Jeph's pistol onto his lifeless body and brought his shoe down on the black ash of the cigarette, finally extinguishing the man's second chance. What a waste. If only he'd had the vision to see the bigger picture.

"GAH!"

Ruse spun and saw the flashes first, followed by the sound of deflected bullets skittering across the floor around him.

The Bad Moons had arrived, along with his sister.

A quick scan for Arthur found the man engaged in combat with Simmons. The big man had pulled Arthur off the boy and now the two fiercely exchanged blows as they moved down the tunnel toward the lobby. That left the three remaining Bad Moons and Natalia, all with weapons aimed at him, firing like hell. This needed to end quickly. He couldn't afford to waste too much energy dealing with another annoyance. He'd already spent much more than he would've liked keeping all this gunfire at bay.

The sound of bullets hitting the floor stopped abruptly as Ruse ripped away all the weapons aimed at him and tossed them across the room. The now familiar sensation of heat flared up in the base of his skull around his implant as he tossed all four of his assailants down the passage leading back to the entrance. A bit more focus was required to collapse the end of the tunnel, sealing them out of the room, but he had spent the last few months training this new ability and it was easier than he would've expected. What he didn't expect was the younger Taylor twin to recover quickly enough to dive back into the room amidst the collapsing passage.

Ruse watched the girl land next to the O'Malley boy and pull a pistol from her boot. Shifting his energy from the tunnel to the girl took only a second, but it was almost a second too late. The bullet floated less than an inch from his forehead. Again.

The girl was fast. Accurate. What a waste of potential this one was, just like her brother. He let the slug fall and reached out with Renaissance, grabbing Doc's body, forcing it to conform to his will. He threw her into the metal wall and pushed, watching her scream soundlessly until he felt her lose consciousness, then released. The girl thudded to the ground, hard.

Ruse closed his eyes and sighed deeply. The faint sounds

of conflict that could be heard from elsewhere in the building were now only a whisper. Like rain on a window. He moved to the center of the room and summoned his full awareness. Raising his arms, he reached out toward each of the pipes that encircled the large room, focusing on their contents, and he began to push.

He'd practiced this. He'd done the assessment. Knew exactly how much pressure he'd need to build for the reservoir to give. He felt the fluid in the pipes stop for a moment, then reverse direction under his guidance, flowing back into the reservoir. At this level of exertion, it didn't take long for his implant to really start burning. A searing agony radiated from the base of his skull as he strained, and blood began to trickle from his nose.

He relished the pain. It was a necessary suffering, like all the wreckage around him.

The suffering required to change the world.

19
THE LAST TIME, I PROMISE

"DOC!"

Marisha slammed against the rubble of the destroyed tunnel, pushing with everything she had, but the debris wouldn't budge. She stopped, breathing heavily and watched JT continue the fruitless effort next to her.

"AH!"

Natalia's scream echoed into the passage. She must have followed Simmons and Rook into the lobby. The Bad Moons exchanged a quick glance, then took off toward the woman's cry. Rounding the corner, they found the entrance to the facility in shambles. Some of the fighting between the crews had spilled into the lobby from the opposite hallway and as a result, the far side of the room was littered with bodies.

"You fucking traitor," Natalia said through gritted teeth. Arthur Rook had the woman on her back on top of the long desk, barely a few feet from the dead guard who was strewn across it. Simmons was unconscious in the corner of the room closest to them, curled up against the splinters of a fallen cabinet. The man was alive, but he looked to be in rough shape, bleeding from many knife wounds peppered across his body. "How could you betray Cain? Why—AHH!"

The man squeezed Natalia's shin where the bone was jutting out at a nauseating angle. "Fuck." Tears streamed from the woman's eyes as she breathed through the pain. "You have always been a sad, pathetic lapdog," she spat, looking Rook in the eyes.

The man leaned further over her, bringing his face close to hers. "And *you've* always been an entitled little brat, *Miss Natalia*." He brandished his knife up high, getting ready to bring it down on her.

JT slammed into his legs first, throwing Rook off his feet before the knife could find Natalia. Marisha pounced on the man as he tumbled to the ground, grabbing the hand that held the knife. It took a few seconds of wrestling and smashing Rook's knuckles against the ground, but eventually the blade came loose and slid across the floor, disappearing under one of the bodies on the far side of the room. A frustrated Rook kicked JT in the teeth, removing her from his legs, and threw Marisha off of him. They all scrambled to their feet, except Natalia who slid off the desk with a grunt and began dragging herself slowly over to Simmons in the corner. Rook paced in front of them, shaking out his wrist and running his hand through his short, slicked back hair.

"The Bad Moon Crew. No King left to lead you," the man said with a cruel smirk.

"Wrong, asshole," JT said, getting up. "The Bad Moon King is right in front of you." She pointed to Marisha next to her. The man's smirk widened into a smile at this. "You wanna get rid of us, you'll have to cross us *all* off. To the very last." The young girl spat blood onto the floor and wiped her mouth. "Shoulda done it at The Hollow when you had the chance."

Rook stopped pacing and steadied himself. "Well, let's not make that mistake again."

The swelling silence overwhelmed Derby once again. He stood, back here, in the endless white. Waiting. Seconds, days, years, for the nothingness to blur and the strange door to take form. As the frame finally crystalized along with the pink glow that surrounded it, fully defining the shape, he hesitated.

What if this was dying? Though it was a faint echo here, he recalled the sound of a gunshot. And the sense of calm he felt about this place, the complete absence, all drawing him through the door. If he opened it, would he be able to return?

In the end, the pull of the void won out, and he resigned himself to moving forward. He reached out and the vast white gave way to the weight of his hand, until it didn't. Feeling the shape inside the frame, soft to the touch, but tangible still, Derby pushed.

DING.

A bell above the door rang as it opened into The Hollow. Or, at least, a hazy version of the diner, with all the same corners and edges. Derby stepped into the familiar room, the pink glow of the sign outside shining through the windows. The space was empty except for one other person. Sitting at the big table, in the center of the dining area, was Cain Gamble.

Rook rushed in. And he was fast.

Marisha barely had a chance to react before she had taken a blow on the chin. The man kicked, interrupting an attack from JT, catching the young girl in the gut and causing her to double over. Marisha was able to return the favor with her own strike, but Arthur took the shot with a smirk and continued his assault.

The fading light of the evening sky poured in through the open doorway of the facility casting their conflict in auburn resolution. The Gamble bodyguard was able to match them step for step, as if their outnumbering him counted for nothing. It was extremely difficult to hit the man; he was never where he should've been. His legs were playing the game two moves ahead of his body, always carrying him into the right positions to do damage and avoid taking it in return. Unfortunately, the Bad Moons did not have the same advantage and very quickly, that damage began to accumulate.

Marisha felt her nose break from the impact of a nasty elbow, followed by a kick to the midsection which sent her reeling backwards to the floor. The world spun as she lay there feeling the taste of copper concentrate in the back of her throat. Her right eye must have been almost swollen shut, as only a sliver of light made it through on that side.

She turned her head, and her obstructed gaze fell on JT who lay a few feet away, a steady flow of blood leaking from the girl's freshly broken nose as well, a film of red staining her teeth. Marisha tried to force herself to stand but the pain was immense. She tilted her head up and found Rook standing there, a satisfied smirk on his face, looking barely inconvenienced. A few scuffs and welts here or there but nothing too far out of place. She would have to fix that.

Suddenly, JT let out an ear-piercing shriek and rushed the man. Despite being visibly startled, Arthur maintained his composure and was able to easily fend off the girl's sloppy advances.

Marisha began the slow process of battling to her feet.

As Rook began to return attacks, JT was quick enough to slip between the danger and jump on the man, wrapping her legs around his waist, bringing her face in line with his. With a crazed look in her eyes, the girl brought her blood-stained teeth together wildly on whatever chunk of flesh was nearest. The vicious bite found a home on the man's right eyebrow. He yelled out in pain as JT clamped down, breaking the skin. Arthur reached up and grabbed the girl by her hair, yanking her head back which brought with it half of his eyebrow and a thick strip of flesh off the side of his face.

The man grunted through gritted teeth and slammed his head forward into the girl's already broken nose, then threw her hard across the room where she crashed into one of the tall cabinets that flanked the desk. The violent impact caused the heavy furniture to fall forward on top of her.

"JT!" Marisha yelled, having made her way back to an unsteady stance. Arthur stood between her and the girl, the right half of his face now a mess of gore. The smirk he had been wearing up till now was gone; the man had murder in his eyes. The edges of the room blurred as Marisha swayed across from him, but she needed to cling to consciousness. She needed to make the bastard pay. For King. For Marv. For all of it.

"Mr. Gamble?"

"Hey, kid." Cain sat tall at the table, his beard full, his eyes the piercing blue that Derby remembered from the last time they met, not the vacant white windows that had looked out from the shell of a man being held captive at Gamble House.

Derby walked further into The Hollow. It was the place that he knew, there was no doubt. But it also wasn't quite right. The greens had a bit too much yellow in them, the pinks were too white. It was The Hollow as you might imagine it, in your mind, in a memory. Almost, but not quite.

"What is this place?" Derby asked as he approached the table. "It's The Hollow but. . .what is it really?"

Cain shrugged. "Wish I could tell ya. I've only been here a minute myself," he said looking around the room distantly. "Or maybe a lifetime. It's hard to tell." His eyes fell back to Derby. "I saw you passing by through the window there, so I tapped on it, called out to ya. Guess you heard me," he said with a smile.

"I guess so," Derby replied. He eyed the chair directly across from Cain, the one that King usually sat in, before pulling a seat over from one of the other tables and sitting off to the side. Cain shifted his gaze between the empty seat in front of him and Derby, thoughtfully running his hand through his beard.

"I knew Obo my entire life," Cain said. "He was just as much a brother to me as Ruse was, if not more. I think Ruse always hated that." A flash of guilt flickered across the man's face. "Needless to say, I knew Obo well. As well as anyone, 'cept for maybe Marisha. And I can say with confidence that he thought a lot of you, Sticks." He smiled.

"I've heard that," Derby nodded. ". . .I can't imagine why," he said, looking down.

"I can," Cain said thoughtfully. "You're someone that carries a lot of hurt around. You wear it on your skin. Obo was the same. Hard to tell, I know. Somewhere amidst the muck and mud of our lives he found a way to reckon with his baggage. To live with it and just. . .*be.*" Cain looked Derby in the eyes. "I think he saw that potential in you, kid. Just like he did the rest of his Bad Moons. And that's all Obo wanted for those around him. Hell, for the whole city. For people to just be. Without the need for permission of any kind. Not from the Fifth, or from each other, or even from their own pain." He smiled, shaking his head. "He was a dreamer, no doubt."

Derby considered the man's words. "Why are you telling me this? Why am I here?" he asked softly.

Cain's face grew serious. "Because I need your help to stop my brother. And I need you to trust me."

Marisha was nowhere near as fast as him, especially not in her current state, but Arthur was angry now. She could use that.

She attacked, knowing that he'd beat her to the position, that his legs would get him there first. Rook easily avoided her strike, planted his feet, and fired back. Marisha took the punch, and pain blossomed across her face. It was a hard shot, just as she had hoped it would be. She was counting on Rook to sit on his attack, to really try to hurt her, putting all his weight on his planted front foot so that when she stomped down on the man's knee, it had nowhere to go but to hell.

The man's scream split the air as his joint folded in the wrong direction. Marisha followed Rook down as he fell to the ground, half falling herself, but managing to maintain control and capitalize on the gaping hole she had just blown in the man's defenses. He barely had time to hit the floor before she was on top of him, raining down blows, slowly rearranging his face.

"Marisha. . ."

The high of revenge was so intoxicating that Marisha didn't hear the girl cry out weakly from across the room.

"Marisha!"

The second, slightly louder shout also fell on deaf ears as Marisha felt the man's orbital bone give out under her elbow. She paused. The bastard was smiling. Through a mouth full of blood, Rook taunted her. The white of his teeth, poking through the red, daring her to finish the job.

"Maman!"

This time, JT's voice, though still thin, broke through the fog of Marisha's rage and she looked up. The girl was stuck under the heavy cabinet, struggling to breathe. Marisha glanced back down at the broken man beneath her, still smiling in the face of defeat, inviting her to continue.

She pushed herself up to her feet and stumbled over to JT. The girl was gasping for air under the dense wood. Marisha summoned up most of the strength that remained in her body and lifted the cabinet, at least enough that JT could slide out from underneath. The young girl's breathing was still frantic and ragged. A few of her ribs had gone and the broken nose certainly made matters more difficult.

"Breathe, JT," Marisha said, stabilizing the girl in her lap. "It's okay, just breathe girl. I got you."

A scuffling across the room drew Marisha's gaze. Arthur was leaning against the doorway of the facility, his face a swollen, gory mess, his left leg completely useless, yet somehow a sickening smile took shape on the man's face as he hobbled slowly out of the Hydro and into the deep orange dusk of the world.

"I need you to trust me."

Derby smiled. "Yeah, well, it's not like I really have options." He stared at Cain for a moment. "How do you know what's going on out there anyway?"

"Seems that I know what Ruse knows," Cain said, looking around the diner. "Something to do with this place, that implant in his head, with Renaissance. . .it's all one big body. We're barely a limb." The man looked distant for a moment and then turned to Derby, his blue eyes burning bright. "He needs to be stopped."

Derby nodded. "What your brother's doing, what he's already done, it's all wrong. *Very* wrong. But The Fifth? The Uppers? He's not wrong about that."

"Of course he's not," Cain said, shaking his head. "But does that justify anything that's happened? What's about to happen?"

"No," Derby replied firmly.

"Even if you could look past the atrocities," Cain continued, "it just won't work. The people of The Reeds are broken. Their rebellion needs to start within." He paused for a moment, looking contemplative. "They need a quiet revolt. One that shapes them to believe they're *deserving* of agency. *That* version of Reed City could grow beyond the shadow of

The Uppers." He looked at the empty chair across from him, "That's what King believed we could build."

Derby breathed deep, meeting Cain's eyes. "How do we stop him?"

"You started it when you came in here. And you'll finish it when you leave. When you walk out that door, I'll be able to follow. In a way. But we won't have long. And I'll need you to let me in."

"Let you in?"

Cain smiled. "I'm just following the thread here, kid. I'm not exactly sure what's gonna happen." His gaze drifted back to King's empty chair. "A friend once told me that we had all the power we needed, we were just holding on too tight to let it through." He looked back at Derby. "Maybe that's how we do this. Maybe it's just about getting out of the way." He shrugged.

Derby sighed and stood up. "Well, let's do it then." He walked across the diner and paused just before the door, turning back.

"Nothing."

Cain turned in his seat and gave Derby a look of mild confusion.

"When we met. . .before. You asked me what I needed,

something I didn't already have. I told you I didn't have a good answer."

"Ah," Cain said.

"I should have said 'nothing'. I couldn't see it then but, looking back, it was all right there. I had all the pieces I needed to. . .to *be.*"

Cain smirked. "I think you still might, kid."

Derby turned and put his hand on the door.

"Hey," Cain said, "do me a favor would ya? Tell my sister that I love her. And that I'm sorry. Sorry that she's always had to clean up after Ruse and I." His eyes shone with a sad acceptance. "Tell her this'll be the last time, I promise." He winked.

Derby nodded.

DING.

He pulled open the door, and exited the place that was almost The Hollow, stepping back into the endless white.

20
CONSEQUENCE

DERBY OPENED HIS eyes and found himself in the midst of a storm. Bodies littered the floor of the room, the passage behind him had collapsed, and in the center of it all stood Ruse Gamble, arms outstretched, and blood trickling from his nose as he pushed on the world.

The massive pipes that crowned the room shuddered under the strain of Ruse's will. Pressure built up in the steel veins as he continued to urge the flow of water inside them backwards, toward the reservoir, where there was no longer room for displacement. As Derby got to his feet, he noticed Doc lying nearby, unconscious but breathing; he could almost feel her chest moving up and down in a steady rhythm.

Returning his attention to the man in the middle of the room, Derby started to move, and as he did, his own footsteps thundered in his ears. He could smell the blood leaking from Ruse's nose, the hot steel scent that filled the room burned his nose, and the blue light that blazed from the man's implant hurt his eyes; it was as if some big dial on the world had been turned up.

Despite his hyperawareness, Derby couldn't shake a nagging presence in the back of his mind. Just as his attention was drawn to it, he realized it was Cain. He could feel him in the wings of his consciousness. Just behind the curtain. The truth behind the elder Gamble's words was clear now, it really was all one big body, and they were both a part of it.

Guided by instinct or by influence, Derby reached out as he crossed the room, mirroring Ruse's posture, and commanded the flow in the pipes to stop. The water obeyed.

Ruse looked up, confusion and rage colliding on his face, blue light roaring brightly from behind his ear, and Derby felt the man redouble his efforts. Not only was holding this renewed wave of force at bay easy, but Derby also found himself able to counteract Ruse's will, to move the water in the opposite direction, slowly relieving the pressure on the system. Though this feat didn't feel difficult, it still exacted a physical toll and Derby felt blood begin to run from his nose. Only, his face was dry. And the smell of copper was not mingled with the scent of hot steel from The Hydro but instead, the blood smell mixed with the dust and abandon of Gamble House.

The body was at war with itself, and Cain Gamble had made sure he was the sacrificial limb.

Derby continued forward, moving closer to the center of the room, the flow in the pipes following him. Ruse opened his mouth suddenly, releasing a scream that Derby barely heard, and expending all of his energy into a push that Derby barely felt. The part of him that played host to Cain Gamble, the piece that stood just offstage, could feel the sheets of the hospital bed at Gamble House, and could feel red life gushing, from every place which it could escape.

As Derby approached the eye of the storm, he paused, examining the man who stood there, who was now leaking from every opening on his face, and he found defeat. It crept in behind the painful red of the man's bloodshot eyes, and the once fearsome tyrant of Reed City now seemed so small. In that moment, when he pushed on the world with every ounce of strength he could muster, and instead of surrendering, the world pushed back, Ruse Gamble gave up.

The man fell to his knees, the blue light that seared behind his ear was extinguished, and the room became still. The pipes above settled into the silence, the flow inside them returning to its natural state. Ruse looked up at Derby and shook his head; face covered in the red remnants of his struggle.

"How?" he whispered, his voice torn to shreds from the strain. He bowed his head and croaked out a weak laugh, speaking raggedly "My luck. . ."

Derby stepped forward. "No," he said quietly. He could feel Cain rapidly losing presence, beginning to slip away. "Luck is small, Ruse. This is consequence." He reached behind the man's ear and felt the circular edges of the implant that was buried there. Then, feeling a final pulse of Renaissance, he forced his fingers underneath the device and pulled hard, ripping it from Ruse's neck.

Ruse cried out and, in that instant, Derby felt the world shrink and dim. Cain was gone entirely; any connection he had felt to something deeper was severed. All at once the world was quieter. Pain suddenly flared, like an old friend, radiating up his arm from his bandaged wrist, and he stumbled backward, dropping the implant.

Ruse looked up, an unsettling sight, red tears streaming from his eyes. "You're going to *rot* here," the man hissed, his voice barely able to push out a whisper. "In the *dirt*, and the *shit*, under their boots. And you'll deserve it, all of you. I could've brought something better, something—" *BANG.*

Derby flinched as Ruse dropped to the ground, fresh red leaking from a new hole in the side of his head where the bullet had gone through. He turned and found Doc propped up against the wall holding her pistol, wincing as she got to her feet. Derby ran over to her, helping the girl steady her balance.

"I'm fine, Sticks," she said, looking at him with a weak smile. "Thanks."

Derby and Doc stood together for a moment, looking around the room and at each other, allowing their minds to catch up with their bodies. Eventually, they each took one final look at the messy corpse of Ruse Gamble, lying among the fallout of his ambition, and headed out of the room through the unblocked passage.

They emerged from the tunnel and found the lobby was almost as much of a wreck as where they came from. The smell of blood and bullets hung heavy in the air, a smell that should've made Derby choke, but recent exposures had left him calloused.

"JT!" Doc called out and they ran over to their friends who were huddled together in the far corner of the room.

"She's gonna be okay," Marisha said, still cradling the girl, who was pale and winced with every breath.

Natalia sat a few feet away, one of her legs jutting out at an odd angle, managing a painful looking position to lean over the unconscious body of Simmons and apply pressure to one of the man's many wounds. "Ruse?" she asked.

Doc nodded slowly. "Done."

"fuck yeah…," JT croaked faintly, giving a weak smile that almost immediately turned into a grimace.

"Is he gonna be alright?" Derby asked, nodding toward Simmons.

Natalia shook her head. "I don't know. He's lost a lot of blood. They both need help," she said looking at JT. "I need one of you to check the guard for a radio," she gestured to the desk behind them, and the body of the uniformed man that was draped over it. Derby rushed over to the desk and patted the body down, eventually leaning carefully over the blood-soaked surface and finding a portable clipped to his belt.

"You all need to leave," Natalia said, grabbing the radio that Derby brought to her. "Get her back down to The Reeds, to the clinic, quick as you can."

"What about you and Sim?" Doc asked.

"We can't move him," Natalia said. "I need help to come here. I'm gonna radio the A's and you're gonna be nowhere near this place when they show up."

"Nat," Marisha interjected, "we're not leaving you to deal with the A's alone."

Natalia looked at Marisha intensely. "Maman. This is *my* family's mess. I'll handle it." She shrugged. "Besides with you lot gone, the story writes itself. My brother lost his mind, The Black Ashes tried to stop him," she gestured to the bodies strewn across the room. "No need for the A's to make an example if no one's left who knows what happened." Marisha looked at Natalia expectantly. "Don't worry about me. I trust that they'll *love* the idea of sending me back to The Reeds hopelessly indebted to them." She smirked confidently, but Derby could see doubt there.

Marisha opened her mouth to protest.

"Please, Maman. He's running out of time."

Marisha hesitated for a moment. "Fuck." She stood, gently lifting JT off the ground. "Thank you, Nat." She nodded to the only remaining Gamble sibling, and the Bad Moons headed for the door. They heard the click of the radio, and Natalia's call for help behind them as they exited the Hydro, welcoming the much fresher air of the crisp, faded evening.

The elevator doors slid open, and the Bad Moons piled into the big glass box. Derby hit the button inside that closed the doors behind them and started their slow journey down the side of the cliff.

Marisha lowered herself to the floor with JT. The girl's breathing had steadied but she was still very pale and very quiet. Derby slid down the elevator wall until he hit the floor, arms resting on his knees in front of him, taking in the view through the tall glass. Doc followed suit next to him.

The Reeds sprawled wide below them, sky blazing orange over the city as the sun cut into the horizon. Tithe would be finishing about now and the crowd that was gathered in The Drum was only a dense cluster of dots from here. Derby thought about the Fifth Council, somewhere in that bunch of dots, so large in name, but from this vantage, no bigger than any others.

He felt Doc's shoulders begin to shake gently beside him; felt her head rest on his shoulder. Derby was surprised to find that he too had tears streaked across his cheeks. They had come on silently, and without his permission. Doc sniffed and sighed deeply, becoming still once again. Derby held his hand out in front of her, rubbing his fingers against his thumb, then letting his palm lay open.

Doc stifled a chuckle and reached into the pouch on her belt, pulling out a coin and placing it into Derby's outstretched hand. He spun the coin around in his fingers a few times before pocketing it as the elevator dropped below the tree line of the northern greenbelt, delivering them back to The Reeds.

21
YOU'RE HERE NOW

TWO WEEKS LATER

"YEAH, THAT HURTS."

The back of Derby's hand burned as the device drew lines across it. The pain was bearable but intensified every time Marisha ran the tool over a particularly bony section of skin.

"Don't be a baby," JT said from across the table where she sat with her feet tucked up on the chair underneath her.

Doc smirked, wrapping her freshly inked hand with a clear bandage. "That's funny, I remember you tearing up when we did yours."

“Oh, shut up, D—” The girl started to jump up from her seat but quickly winced and sat back down holding her side.

Doc chuckled. “That’s handy.” JT stuck her tongue out threateningly.

“Almost done, Sticks,” Marisha said. “You holding up okay?”

Derby nodded. “I’m good.”

They were back in the Bad Moon apartment. It had taken them a couple days to put everything back to how it was before the A’s had turned the place over. In all of the material ways, they had been able to set their home right. The furniture all sat in its proper arrangement, the broken front door had been replaced with a new one, and music flowed from the HAM radio in the corner, just the way it used to. But as he sat there, letting his mind wander to avoid acknowledging the pain in his hand, Derby couldn’t help but see the apartment the same way that he had seen the slightly crooked version of The Hollow that he found on the other side of nothing: almost, but not quite.

That was this version of The Bad Moon Crew’s home. It had its old skin back, but there were things missing here that couldn’t be replaced, couldn’t simply be put back in order.

“Born Under a Bad Sign, Albert King, 1967,” Doc said as a new melody filled the air, pulling Derby out of his thoughts.

He tilted his head, looking at Doc. “I thought you hated the blues.”

The girl shrugged. "Times change, Sticks." She smiled, unconsciously touching the bandage on her hand that covered fresh lines of black forming the shape of a record. The same tattoo Marv had worn under his skin.

"Alright, you're done," Marisha said, turning off the device, silencing the dim buzz, and giving Derby his hand back. He inspected the image that Marisha had buried there: two branches crossing each other at the ends.

JT looked up at him, grinning widely. "Look at you, Sticks. You got ink. Never thought I'd see the day."

He shrugged. "Yeah, well. . .times change, I guess," he said with a smirk.

Doc walked over and began tightly binding his hand with the same clear wrap that she was wearing. Her eyes grew serious as she finished securing the bandage. "I think I'm gonna go for a visit," she said.

The rest of the group exchanged quick, surprised glances.

"You wanna come with?" Doc asked, intercepting Derby's gaze.

He couldn't avoid being startled by the question. "You. . .want the company?"

Doc smiled. "That's why I asked."

"Sure. Yeah, of course."

"Great." She tugged her hood up quickly, pulling it tight around her face and made for the front door.

"Be careful," JT said. "Maman and I were there this morning and saw a bunch of A's creeping around up north."

Marisha shook her head as she began loading a bag with cooking utensils. "The A's are *not* after us anymore, JT. They always increase their presence on Feast. And especially after The Hydro. . ."

The young girl shrugged. "They're still a bunch of assholes. Just be careful."

"We will," Derby said.

"No later than three at The Drum please, you two," Marisha said. "We start serving at five-thirty."

Doc opened the door, holding it wide and ushering Derby into the hallway. "We'll be there," she said, peeking back into the apartment before closing the door behind them.

Rain lightly peppered their hoods and the ground around them, giving the grassy spaces between the plots a wet sheen.

"How're you doing?" Derby asked gently.

"I'm good, actually," Doc replied. "I thought it would hurt

more. But it just hurts the same." They stood at the southern edge of the cemetery where King and Marv's headstones had been placed. The graves were decorated with flowers, and the surrounding area was flooded with tributes. "If there's any extra pain, it's mostly from the guilt that I haven't been here yet. I mean, look at all this." She pulled her hood tighter around her face. "I'm probably the last person in The Reeds to visit at this point."

Derby shrugged. "You're here now," he said. His gaze wandered down the hill to the east, toward the far corner of the graveyard where the tall tree stood. "When I lost Etta, I. . .coming here would've made it real, I guess? I couldn't stand the thought of that. But I think I was just squeezing. Trying to hold on, stay in control." He breathed deeply, shaking his head. "That's exhausting."

Doc nodded. "Yeah."

They stood in silence for a while, rain and tears mingling on Doc's face. "We should go," she said eventually. The girl stepped forward and ran her hand along King's headstone, then crouched for a minute, closing her eyes, beside Marv's grave. After a few moments, she stood and made room for Derby who approached the plots of the fallen Bad Moons, crouching between them. He shifted his gaze between the two graves and sighed, reaching into his pocket, and pulling out a coin. The same one that Doc had given him on the elevator. He placed the coin against the base of Marv's headstone.

“Mon chéri.”

They turned toward the new voice behind them.

“Nat,” Doc said, embracing the woman. Natalia was wearing her usual dark outfit and supporting her weight with a cane on the side of her injured leg. As always, the girl was shadowed by Simmons.

Doc looked at the large man, mildly surprised. “Sim, it’s good to see you up and about.”

“Miss Taylor,” Simmons said, bowing his head slightly. “An achievement I owe, in no small part, to the both of you and your colleagues.”

Doc smiled, then turned back to Natalia. “Listen, Nat, I know we haven’t had much of a chance to talk since The Hydro but thank you. For everything. Having our home back, walking freely around the city again. . .we owe you.”

Natalia waved the girl off. “Please, Doc. I owe you as much, if not more.” Her eyes wandered to the pair of headstones that stood behind the Bad Moons. “You know, when your brother and I first started seeing each other, we went to great lengths to keep it secret, for obvious reasons,” she smirked. “But King knew. From the very beginning. I’m still not sure how, but he knew. And no matter how close they were, he never told my brother. I don’t even think he told Maman.” She shook her head slowly. “So, when we finally decided to share our ‘secret’,

King acted just as surprised as anyone. That secret was ours, and he let us keep it." She paused, shifting her gaze back to the group around her.

"What King was trying to build here, him and Cain, *that's* ours now. So, whatever we think we owe to each other, let's pay it to them. To the city."

Doc smiled. "We will. On that note we should head down to The Drum. We promised Maman we wouldn't be late."

Natalia nodded. "See you down there," she said.

As Doc turned to leave, Derby spoke. "Miss Gamble." He paused as Natalia eyed him expectantly. "Your brother. Cain. He, uh. . .I. . ." Derby rubbed his neck in discomfort, then found Natalia's eyes. "He loved you. And he's sorry. For the mess."

She tilted her head, and a wave of curiosity broke across her face for a moment before she fixed Derby with a stare and the ghost of a smile. "Thank you, Mr. O'Malley."

The Bad Moons turned and made for the entrance of the cemetery, leaving Natalia Gamble to pay her respects.

"It wasn't *that* weird, was it?" Derby asked as they walked through the busy streets of the northern Reeds, enjoying a break in the rain.

"Giving the girl a message from her dead brother?" Doc asked. "Nah, more like. . .mildly uncomfortable." She winked.

Derby smiled, shaking his head.

"It's not like you could've explained it anyway," Doc continued, "not without sounding totally insane."

"I still don't understand most of it," Derby said. "It was so vivid at first but it's faded now, like someone else's memory."

They continued into the city heading for The Drum at the heart of it.

"Well, I wouldn't worry about it too much, Sticks. It might've been nice for her actually," Doc said. Derby's brow furrowed at this. "Hearing someone else say his name. Reminding her that he's not forgotten. That he's still here, in that way at least."

Derby considered the girl's words and slowed to a stop just in front of a narrow alley. "I'll meet you down there."

Doc looked back at him, head tilted. "All good?"

"Yeah. Just something I need to take care of."

She continued looking hesitant.

"Three o'clock. I promise," he said.

Doc shrugged. "Don't be late."

He nodded and headed down the nearby alleyway.

Derby's watch read quarter past two by the time he made it downtown. The city core was always a bustle of activity ahead of Feast, and Paisley Street was no exception. Shop owners ran around preparing their carts to set up in or around The Drum, and a general volume of people mingled about, slowly making their way to the center of the city for the coming festivities.

As he walked down the street toward the short, narrow shop that was sandwiched between two taller structures, Derby's hands developed a sweaty film, and his heart sped up. His body was rejecting what he was asking it to do. Trying to protect him from the perceived danger on the inside of the small building. But he moved forward anyway, doing his best, with each step, to get out of his own way.

He paused for a moment as he reached the door, and for a brief instant, he thought he saw Etta's face reflected in the glass. Taking a deep breath, and shaking his head clear, Derby entered the shop.

"Ho, I thought everyone would be heading to The Drum by now, you're the first—"

Otis fell silent, as he looked up from the countertop he was scrubbing, and his eyes found Derby standing in the doorway. They stood there in the silence for what felt like a long while.

Derby had so many things he wanted to say, all running on a confusing loop in his head, but he couldn't get his mouth to form the shape of the words for any of it.

Otis walked out from behind the counter and approached him, but Derby was still unable to make a sound. He stood in front of the older man, Etta's father, muted by his anxiousness, but found a strange sense of comfort. Relief that he had simply walked through the door.

Otis looked at him and, tears crystalizing around the edges of his eyes, pulled him into a voiceless embrace. Derby hugged the man back.

REED CITY

Written by GHOSTI

Thanks For Reading.

www.iwasghosti.com

www.ingramcontent.com/pod-product-compliance
Lightning Source LLC
LaVergne TN
LVHW091114080826
845145LV00008B/1909

9781067416904